*This Train is For*

Bernie McGill

NO ALIBIS PRESS

First published in 2022
by No Alibis Press

Printed by TJ Books, Padstow

Front cover: Rory Jeffers
Typesetting/book design: Stephen Connolly
Author photo: Jonathan Ryder

A CIP record for this book
is available from the British Library

HARDBACK ISBN 978-1838108120
PAPERBACK ISBN 978-1838108175

2 4 6 8 10 9 7 5 3 1

*for May*

# CONTENTS

# This Train is For

Coleraine, *nook of ferns*, 8:19 a.m. Eighty-seven minutes to go.

The flatlands, the North-East Liberties, the Lower Bann twisting out of sight to the west. To the north, Bellasses, Ballyclabber; to the south, Lodge, Mountsandel, Wattstown. The old names preserved in townlands and parishes, the history of the place written light, spoken low, so only the alert will hear. You'll see few of these names on street signs. You have to start with the old maps, with the records of the engineers of the Ordnance Survey, then go further back again to decode the anglicisations, the translations, the scribal errors, the renamings. To excavate the old stories.

And so he goes, in cap disguising thinning hair, and with aching, creaking bones; in failing eyesight, and hearing that lately has begun to miss the softer tones in Helen's voice. The train leaves behind the cast iron fretwork of the station, the pennanted wooden fascia. Tullans, Windy Hall, Knockantern, Loughanreagh, Fish Loughan, Coolderry, MacFinn. This is what it feels like to travel through history. This is what we do here: move forward while facing back, keeping a sharp eye on what has been, in case it gets a run on us, overtakes on our blind side.

Forty years of poring over maps at County Hall, the building out of sight now, beyond the old black stone bridge. Forty years of settling appeals, of policy decisions on ribbon development, replacement dwellings, disputed boundaries, rights to privacy, loss of light. Forty years of watching as town boundaries creep along the coast, grow inland, merge almost into one, and all that time distracted by the rhythms, by the music and the meanings of the place names. Here, the entrance to the ford; here, the plain of the small hills; here, the abandoned lime kilns; the grey lake; the back of the oak wood, the townland of the son of Finn. Tracing a line always back to the home place, to the place of the hearth.

'I'll come with you,' Helen had said, and then, 'Conor could meet us off the train.' Any excuse for a chance to see the grandson, but it's better that he goes alone. None of this makes any sense to Conor. His generation doesn't understand theirs and that's the way it should stay. It's hard to be brave when brave is not something you feel you've ever been but he is trying, one station at a time. He would board the train, he told himself. If he changed his mind, he could get off at any stop. He could cross the tracks and wait for the incoming train. He could go back the way he had come, back to Helen, back to never hearing what it was his sister wanted to say to him.

Under the road at ASDA, the back of the hospital, the industrial estate. The sun just above the horizon, beginning to tint the clouds. A clump of trees around Damhead. Cattle sheltering under a hedge. A burn crossing under; a road crossing over the tracks. The December moon lacy white, still hanging, overlooked, overlooking, in the sky.

He wouldn't dream of driving all the way to the city now, not with the traffic the way it is, not when it's free for him to travel by train. He used to love a run out in the car, had the first one on their road, a black Morris Minor at a time when only the doctor was behind the wheel. He was earning good money, his first job with the Council. He didn't tell them at home that he was going to the car dealers and when he drove down the lane, with Helen for the first time, his mother was standing, white-faced at the window, a hand over her mouth. She thought it was bad news that was driving towards her. She thought that someone had taken ill.

The conductor walks through the carriage. 'Does anyone need tickets?' he says, but immediately afterwards: 'You all have them.' He gives the answer in an aside, uttered under the breath. He wants to make it clear that he's not checking tickets. He doesn't want you to stop him unless you're buying. He's a busy man. What was that thing his mother used to say? 'Here's your hat. What's your hurry?' A push to leave; an invitation to stay. Contradictory messages, pulling you both ways. You should go. Don't leave us. (Leave *her*.) Stay.

A pause at Ballybrakes. The speckled townland, or town of the badgers, depending on which interpretation you favour. Once a name is tampered with, there's a risk of it losing its meaning, or its meaning changes, or is no longer relevant, or comes to mean something else instead. Language is fluid. It cannot be fixed. Something is gained and lost in the usage, a deposition here, an erosion there, a loosening of hold. There is no denying the strength of words, their power to injure, the impossibility of taking back what is uttered once it has gone from the mouth. The undulations and abrasions caused. The altered landscape formed of the tongue.

Outside, retail units, metal fencing, sewage pipes running parallel to the lines. And now the Victorian-built station, the brick below the platform leaching lime.

Ballymoney, *townland of the bog*, 8:32 a.m. Seventy-four minutes to go.

Advertisements for paints and components, corrugations of steel, a new footbridge of ramped concrete and suspended wire against black stone, red brick. Something glints from the hinge of a bin: a bead of water hanging like amber in the weak wintry sun. Over the rooftops a church spire climbs into the sky.

A man steps on to the train, passes him by, slides into a seat further up the carriage. From the man's jacket the smell of wet dog rises.

Carnany, Greenville, Landhead, Cummingstown, Greenshields River culverted under the track. To the west, Long Mountain, to the east Slieveanorra, and further south the hollows of Frosses Bog. Mound of the birds; town of the monks; mountain ridge; the watery, the marshy places. Tweedy colours, moss greens and turf browns, mist rising like a wraith below the dark hills. The yellowing firs. The reddening rowan. A pinking of the sky. Slate roofs. Telegraph wires carrying news.

Lizzie has asked for him. After all this time. He had thought he had no feeling left for his sister, but, 'Please come,' the priest said on the phone, and everything else fell away.

At first Helen said, 'You're not to consider it. Not after everything she said.' But he had insisted that he would go, promised he would come straight back. 'You're not wise,' she said, 'at your age. You're not fit for this.'

'What are you talking about?' he had said to her. 'The doctor said I was a wonder. She said she'd never seen a fitter eighty-three-year-old.'

'You'd think you might have picked up some sense along the way.' Still, she knotted his tie for him. 'I won't have her saying you haven't been well looked after,' she said. A slight twist of her mouth and then, 'That's a bit more Protestant-looking.' She was a mild-mannered woman, Helen, but she was not above delivering the occasional barb all the same. He should never have repeated to her what Lizzie said all those years ago.

The priest on the phone from the hospital had said that Lizzie was near the end. He said she'd had his number in her purse. She could have picked up the phone at any time. Why didn't she? Why hadn't he? Sixty years wasted, out of stubbornness, or bitterness, or righteousness, or aggrievement. And for what? In order to save face? He doesn't know what arrangements she's made, or if she's made any. Lizzie has no heir. She'd take nothing to do with men. She elbowed a lad off his bicycle and into the ditch one night after a dance. She became famous for her vigour in repelling unwanted attention. For all he knew, she could have willed the house and farm to the church. They said the new man was very popular, that he said the mass in twenty minutes. If she had, there was nothing he could do about that, if she'd shut him out till the last. What good is it to you now, said Helen. What good, indeed. Lizzie had had her day of the place and that day, it would seem, was nearing its end. He'd had no material need of it. But to put his hand again on the wood of the door, to pass under the lintel. That'd be something. That'd quicken the pulse. And he found that he was curious. To see it the way she had left it would tell him something of how, all this time, she had lived.

The sheep are beginning to wake now, to gather themselves up from under the hedges. Cattle wait at gates. A bath in a field serves as a feeding trough. Raths and cairns and souterrains to either side of the track.

The yellow plain; Tachartach's cross; the place of the standing stones; the withered wood. Metal silos; a stone archway; a silage mound in a farmyard, weighted down with tyres. The whin, dark, unflowering. A ploughed field, a swarm of drumlins. A fine, white-limed farmhouse, lights in the kitchen, in the yard. Smoke drifting upward from the chimney.

The track cuts through the jagged boundaries of baronies,

parishes, townlands, cuts through the parabolae of minor roads, the vein work of laneways and hedges and ditches, of remembered and disputed rights of way. Bridleways, loanens, pads. Desire paths. Unpaved tracks and trails.

The respite of a small white church, modest, Protestant, a tiny bell tower, gothic windows, and then the rivers, the Maine meeting the Clogh where it crosses at Glarryford. It strikes you when you look at the maps, how many places of worship there are, even for a small place like this. Towers, spires, minarets, domes. Difference is a relative term, like stranger, or other. Different from what, he has often wondered, from whom?

A single red chimney stack, all that remains of a derelict beetling mill; a road crossing; a herd of black sheep in a flooded field, their fleeces reflected back at them, a doubling of the dark.

The conductor passes through. 'Anyone find a purse?' he says. 'Lady has lost a purse.'
The passengers shift their feet, peer below seats.
'That's terrible,' a woman says from behind. 'I hope it's found.'
'Somebody will be away with it,' says the wet dog man from in front.
'It'll bring them no luck,' the woman says.

On the horizon, the smooth hump of Slemish. In the clearing sky nine long-necked geese stretch out towards the east. A tractor parked under a hedge. Scrubland. A piebald in a field. A cluster of wind turbines, white against blue. And beyond them, unseeable from here, the old farmstead, the gravel yard, the red roof of Downey's barn, the place he hasn't set foot in for over sixty years. The name of it, always, in his head, never on his lips.

Cullybackey, *the bend of the river*, 8:51 a.m. Fifty-five minutes to go.

Out there beyond the topiaried hedges grow ash, sycamore and lime, patches of hazel-oak, heather, cotton sedge. Cranberry and crowberry on the bogland; in the grasslands, Irish hare. In the rivers, otter, brown trout, dollaghen. And overhead, curlew, reed bunting, yellowhammer, song thrush. Stone wall boundaries mark the fields that run to the twists and bends of the Maine. People put such faith in walls, for shelter, to mark what is one's own, or what one believes to be owned. To keep trespassers out, to keep livestock in; to defend against floods; to safeguard privacy; to hide; to keep the peace.

They were trespassers themselves as youngsters, he and Lizzie, no respecters of boundaries in those days, hiding out in their neighbour's hay shed. John Wayne and Roy Rogers, building bale barricades against imagined enemies, shooting their way out of an ambush, picking off a gang of outlaws as they rode into town. They were always the good guys. The bad guys were unseen. Things were very clear cut to them then.

They robbed old Downey's apples. He chased them, one

day, roaring after them that he'd strangle them when he caught them, and they ran in to their mother, casting apples as they went, and hid under the oilcloth. He followed them in. 'Have you seen those two renegades?' he said. 'They're after pulling every apple off my tree. They're getting as wild as weasels, Molly.' There was a pause in which they dared not breathe, in which they detected a rustle that may have been the movement of an arm, a finger to the lips, after which Downey's boots, caked with cow dung and straw, made their way across the floor, closer to the table.

'If I get my hands on them,' he shouted, 'I'll pull the guts out of them and shape them into sausages and fry them over the fire for my dinner.'

Lizzie's eyes widened. She clamped a hand over his mouth.

'Are you sure it was them?' they heard Mother say in a voice that he later suspected, may have been stifling a laugh.

'Haven't I two eyes in my head?' said old Downey, overloud again.

'I've seen no word of them since morning. Sit down and take a sup of tea when you're here. The sodas are hot off the griddle.'

They watched as the chair was scraped back and old Downey settled, legs stretched, feet crossed at the ankles, the foul boots inches from their noses. And there they sat, Downey and his mother, going over all the news of the day, from the bad snows they'd had in March to the great summer that had followed after, in no apparent hurry to get on, and old Downey crossing and uncrossing his ankles the whole while, wafting cow dung in their faces. And when he left, finally, and the pair of them crawled out, stiff from not moving, near choking from the smell, and their stomachs growling with hunger, their mother glanced at them once and said, 'Is that where you were? Jim Downey's after your hides.'

They'd been having their fun with the children, he realised later, teaching them a lesson without their knowing. It's like a story from a fairy tale, so long ago is it now, seventy-five years or near enough. It's a strange thing, hindsight. Why is it you can't see the thing clearly in the moment of your living it? Why does it take years of looking back to unpack the meaning?

Ballymena, *the middle townland*, 9:00 a.m. Almost halfway.

Glass block and brown brick at the station. Strip lights reflecting on the glass.

Bags heaped with de-icing salt, the platform winter-ready. That wheel design on the railings must date back to the early 1900s. Strange how some things last, and others don't. Between the barbs of the bird deterrent and the canopy of the station roof, there is a strip of pale sky and further down the line the mostly leafless trees are stark and bare.

'Local bus services are available from this station.'

No smoking.
No trespassing.
No loitering.

Head-phoned and hatted commuters board the train. A

woman sits down beside him, turns her knees to the aisle, talks over to a companion. The draught from the platform chills his ankles. Forty-six minutes to go.

His first job after he left Queen's had been here, in the Planning Service. His mother had always said that a Civil Service job was a great coup for a Catholic. 'And a bad place to find a Catholic wife,' Lizzie said.

'I'm not looking,' he had told her.

'Is that so?' said Lizzie.

'What's wrong with Helen?'

'She seems a civil enough girl.'

'And what?'

Lizzie was silent. She looked at their mother. She'd just come in from the washing line, was standing at the kitchen table, folding pillow slips into a neat pile.

'Could you not find a girl among your own?' Mother said, after a pause. 'There's many a one round here would take you, now that you're earning good money.'

'Nobody round here would be good enough for the university boy,' Lizzie said.

'I'm not interested. I'm marrying Helen.'

Mother's lips pursed. She carried on folding edge to edge and then edge to edge again. 'I heard her father was in the police,' she said.

'Your sources are correct.'

She picked up the laundry, turned away. 'Your father would be turning in his grave.'

Their father was always her trump card. He barely remembered him. A tall man with a pipe, a waft of tobacco smoke, hands chapped and rough from the farm. His parents' wedding photo stood framed on the dresser beside a photo of his father's young brother, Joe. As a boy Joe had gone to stay with cousins in Belfast, got caught up in the trouble in the 1920s, killed by RIC officers on the rampage, in retaliation for the shooting of a colleague. 'Tit for tat' they used to call it: three of yours for one of ours and on and on it went. Exponential grief. They had grown up with the borrowed hurt of Joe's loss, though he was dead long before either Lizzie or he were born. His mother thought that the family history ought to have been enough to steer him away from Helen, but something much stronger had pulled him towards her, and kept them together through the worst of times: through the years of shootings, the bombings, the threats. He thought of Lizzie at the time of the signing of the agreement, wondered what way she had voted, if she had been ready to put her name to peace. At the time Helen had said the rest of the family could call themselves what they liked; she wasn't for giving up her British passport. Then twenty years on, along came Brexit and off she marched one morning to the post office with her Irish passport application. 'I don't want to be in a different queue from the rest of you at the airport,' she said. Practicalities putting paid to allegiances. 'And besides, Mary Ann McCracken would approve.'

'We'll make a United Irelander out of you yet, Granny,' said Conor, with a wink.

She skited a tea towel at him, but she smiled at that. She'd take anything from Conor.

He had seen Lizzie once here, years ago, not long after

he and Helen were married. He was leaving the courthouse where he'd been called to give evidence at a hearing, a dispute over a boundary that had gotten out of hand, and as he came out, he spotted her, heading in towards the ivy-fronted hotel that had been a favourite haunt of their mother's on the rare occasions when she had come to town. Lizzie saw him too. They both stopped, momentarily, and then she turned her head and carried on as if he were a stranger, or someone she'd known once but couldn't place, someone from a long time ago.

Once clear of the red brick the mist thickens. Nothing to be seen now but the outlines of hedges, laneways, the silvering of a burn, black-wrapped bales. The line travels close to the Braid through Harryville and Ballee, meanders away, returns at Slaght, Appletee. Through Sharvogues, the place of bitter herbs, stone pillars, pylons marching across fields.

He is surprised to find that there is a prayer in his head. He isn't much of a one for praying but some things learned young never leave you and there is music in the Memorare, he found. 'Never was it known': the efficacy of the inversion. 'That anyone who fled unto thy protection, implored thy help, or sought thine intercession was left unaided.' The plea of the opportunist—you helped all those others, now please help me. He had met a woman once, an acquaintance of Helen's, a fellow member of her church choir, who said that work was a prayer, and family was a prayer, and love was a prayer. He quoted her often to Helen who occasionally despaired at his lack of faith. This is not a selfless act, this journey. What he is praying for, is the courage to face his sister after all this time.

He said to Helen, after they'd met, 'What will your people say about me?' She was brought up Church of Ireland. She had always been relaxed about the differences in the religions in which they'd each been raised.

'They'll say you're from fine country stock,' she said. 'It's the one God, isn't it? It's how you live your life that matters to me.' Her faith never wavered through all those early years of trying for a child, through the weeks of hope when her body clung to the promise of what could be, the months of despair that followed when the possibility came to nothing in a flood of blood. Only once she had said to him, 'Do you think there's something in it? Do you think it's possible to bring ill on someone by wishing it?' It had pained him to hear her say it, to know that she had remembered, had held that thought in her head all that time. She was better, worthier than that. He quietened her straight away. But he couldn't deny that he'd thought it too, after what Lizzie had said. And then, when they feared it would never happen for them: their beautiful Clara, born on a March day, herald of light, of joy.

Ballylurgan, townland of the long low ridge; Aughalish, yew wood; Drumsough, ridge of berries; Barnish, a gap; Granny, a gravelly place; Kilbegs, the little churches; Dunsilly, fort of the sally tree; Spring Farm, Niblock, Steeple.

Antrim, *a single house or habitation.* 9:14 a.m. Thirty-one minutes to go.

There's more than one house now. Sprawling estates and roundabouts. At the station, cut-out shamrocks in the fascia. On the platform the screens display a list of trains expected or delayed. Anticipation, disappointment: the usual stuff of travelling. Passengers standing in the carriage now, faces merging in the train windows. Where do people work these days? What do they do in those high-rise offices in the city? 'Fin Tech,' Conor said. It made him think of an automated shark, prowling the waters, scenting blood. 'Financial technology, Granda. The global economy. It's where the money is now.' And maybe that was the answer: to lift the young up and out of the places that they'd come from; to set them in jobs in mirrored towers that reflected all the lights of the city, from where they traded facts and figures with other young people in other high-rises in London, in Hong Kong, in New York. The names of the pubs and clubs in those places trip off the tongues of Conor and his friends. They'd be hard pressed any of them to name the townland, the territories that their people came from. He has been wondering, for some time now, if erasure is the price they've chosen to pay for progress.

Moylinny, Muckamore, Ballycraigy, Islandbane, Dunadry where Sixmilewater first appears. They used to dig around here, at Lyle's Hill, close to Templepatrick. A whole group of them on a field study from the university, piled into the professor's van with shovels and trowels and boots. Helen in her overalls, always at the centre of his line of vision, dark curls held back by a yellow scarf, a smut of soil on her forehead from where she'd wiped the back of her hand on her brow. Those were heady days, sharing tea from a flask, packed ham sandwiches, hands caked in dirt. And that day that they came across the man staggering up a country road towards a railway crossing; it must have been close to here. Arms raised, eyes trained upwards, a clutch of followers behind. In his two hands, a divining rod. The professor stood on the van brakes, abandoned the planned dig for an impromptu interview. He could see them there, standing on the road, the professor's big head bowed, listening, as the train rattled on through Cloghanduff, Ballyrobert, Kingsbog, Carntall. At a wave from the prof they stepped out of the van. 'Fall in!' he shouted and they joined the little group, down a muddy lane towards an old metal stile. And then Helen was beside him.

'You first,' he had said.

She glanced back as she passed through, the gate clanking against the shutting post behind her. 'First through the kissing gate,' she had said. 'You'll have to pay the toll.' He still teased her about that. He didn't pay it then but he did later, in the months and years that followed, over and over again.

Mossley West, *clearing by mossy land*, 9:26 a.m. Twenty minutes to go.

On less sure ground here.

Steep banks and brambles, mock Tudor housing, garden furniture and conservatories. Some kind of berry growing from thick ivy in the sidings, still glossy, green. And now the water, a finger of lough, stretching in from the Irish Sea. They are travelling on reclaimed land. To the left, playing fields; a sluggish waterway, barbed wire, sewage pipes. To the right, red signal lights, motorway lanes, slowing traffic. The war memorial on the escarpment at Knockagh Hill is visible for miles to the east overlooking the lough.

Their mother always said that he and Lizzie were as thran as each other. Lizzie was two years older and strong. He remembered the day they were playing down at the river. They called it the river but in summer it was little more than a sheugh, easily wadeable from one bank to the other. They'd built a crossing out of stepping stones they had dug out of the bank, dropped them in one by one. Lizzie had crossed to the opposite side, was making her way back again, but he'd already started from his own bank and refused to turn back. One of them was going in. After a tussle, mid-stream, in they went, the pair of them. They sat on the bank to try to dry out before they headed home, and not a word was spoken. When they finally appeared back at the house, still dripping, griping to their mother, blaming each other, she couldn't hide her smile.

Yorkgate. 9:35 a.m. Eleven minutes.

Cranes, an overpass, spires and towers, motorway signs in blue and white. Scaffolding, yellow cladding, multi-storied car parks and new hotels. The river, glassy, tidal. Graffitied walls, wasteland, the gasworks chimneys, the Lagan. Flags.

City of red brick old and new.

His mother had been proud when the master said he

should try for the grammar school exam, cried the day she packed him off in her cousin's grocery van to Derry. He remembered Lizzie in the doorway, holding back. Then at the last minute, she ran to the window of the van, pressed a little tin box into his hand. Inside, wrapped in her best linen handkerchief, was a whole eggshell she'd blown out, kept from Easter that year. She'd dyed it with beetroot and bilberries and onion skins. It looked like a marble, a jewel. He had kept it for years, protected in its tin, through school and university. The day he left the home place, he set it down on the chest of drawers in his room, crushed it easily with the heel of his hand, left it for Lizzie to find.

Lanyon Place. 9:39 a.m. Seven minutes.

The last time a priest had rung him it was the old man, the one he remembered. That was the time that Mother died. He went to the church, sat near the back, stood away from the grave at the burial. A few old neighbours sought him out, shook his hand, avoided his eye. You'd have thought he had done something shameful, that he had disgraced the family in some way. Lizzie, at the graveside with their cousins, never looked his way once, though she must have known he was there.

Botanic, *for Queen's University & Shaftesbury Square.* 9:44 a.m. Two minutes left to go.

His old stomping ground, his and Helen's: Derryvolgie House, Whitla Hall, dancing in the Harty Room in University Square. Then down on one knee in the shrubbery under her window at Riddel, not caring who heard or saw him. Helen, laughing above him in her blue pleated dress.

'You idiot,' she said. 'Yes, yes, I will.'

The day he told them they'd set a date, there was silence in the house. 'You'll come,' he said. His mother didn't speak. 'You'll come to my wedding, Mother. Lizzie?'

'There's no point in pretending we approve when we don't,' Lizzie said at last.

'Your father,' his mother said, wringing her hands.

'My father what?'

'He wouldn't have wanted the daughter of a policeman setting foot on his land,' Lizzie said.

'Good God, Lizzie. Can you not look forward? What's the matter with you?'

'I'm only saying what Mother is trying to say. Why don't you think about us?'

'It's got nothing to do with you who I marry.'

'It's got everything to do with us. You're the only son, more's the pity. You have a duty to your family.'

'Duty?'

'Yes, duty, though you never see it. Have you forgotten who your people are?'

'Marrying Helen won't change that.'

'Is that what you think? Do you think you'll be able to bring her here and rear your half-breed children among us, and that we won't have anything to say about that?'

'What way is that to talk? Mother, will you speak some sense into her?'

But Mother didn't say anything and then Lizzie said: 'I pray for our sake and for the sake of our line that you have no children with her. I'll pray for that every day.'

'You'll not be troubled by either of us,' he told them and that was the last they spoke.

City Hospital. 9:46 a.m. Final stop.

There's still time to go back, to turn around, to pretend that he was never here. But he finds his feet carrying him up the ramped walkway to the hospital tower, the distinctive yellow brick showing through the trees, and in he goes, through the sliding doors. A lift, a corridor, windows and screens. Smell of disinfectant, porridge. It's too early for visiting hours but they'd said, 'Don't delay. Ring the buzzer. We'll let you in.' And then there's Lizzie, in the metal bed, her hair thinned, white, the bones of her cheeks high, a drip inserted in a pock-marked arm. Her closed eyes, their mother's face from all those years ago. The thin eyelids flicker, open; her eyes fix on his.

'It's you,' she says. And her eyes close again.

He sits down in the chair by the bed and listens to the sounds of the ward: the beeps and the blips, the inflations of the mattress, rattling trolleys, the clink of glass jugs. A nurse, or an auxiliary, offers him tea and he asks about Lizzie and she says she'll see if she can send someone in to speak to him. When she brings the tea, it is milky and sweet. And then he must close his eyes too because the next thing he knows he's back in the home place.

He and Lizzie are hiding out in Downey's hay shed where they've barricaded themselves in with a torch and a copy of *The Dandy*, pool of light on Desperate Dan and Korky the

Cat, and it's growing dark outside. They can hear the cows lowing in the fields and the hens squawking as they settle down to roost, and then their mother's voice calling them in for their supper and they crawl out on their elbows and as they're crossing the yard towards the light at the window, a bat swoops low overhead, and Lizzie shrieks and ducks and stumbles because old Downey has told her that if she goes out after dark, the bats will attack her, catch their claws and their wings in her hair and she'll have to be scalped to get the creatures out again. He catches her by the hand and says, 'It's all right, Lizzie. I've got you.' Nothing is forgotten; it is all stored away, all the hurt that happened, all the words that were said. And he thinks now that it would have been better for them both to have thought harder and to have looked deeper, to have found some other words to say. When he opens his eyes, she is quiet and still and her hand lies in his and it hardly weighs anything at all. And his mouth forms a word and the sound is like the rustle of leaves, like a long drawn out breath, like a sigh: the place of the ash trees, that's what it means, the name of the home place, Ushinagh.

# There is More than One Word

It is late September and the footpaths on Botanic Avenue are treacherous with rain and fallen leaves. Jaynie trundles her suitcase across the road and picks her steps around a puddle at the mouth of a blocked drain close to the kerb. She hears the word 'kerb' in her head and it sounds strange to her. Was that what they had always called it? There was another word, she thinks, from years and years ago, when they used to play 'Kick the tin' out in the front street, but whatever it was, it escapes her now.

She has taken a taxi from the airport, but on a whim, has asked the driver to drop her at a café. Deirdre said she'd leave a key out for her; she won't be back from work for hours. She said she'd phone Jaynie right away if there was any word.

'Take your pick,' the driver said. 'But you needn't be looking for a sandwich. It's all wraps and falafels round here these days.'

She searches for the Canterbury & Dyke but it's gone from the corner of Cromwell Road and when she follows the curve of the street to look for the student flat she'd shared nearly thirty years before, the building is gone as well, replaced by a new apartment block in fresh red brick. The houses to either side retain the arched doorways she remembers, the sash windows crowned with pale coping stones, the narrow brick chimneys with their slim chimney pots. But her old building looks like it has been picked up and shaken, brushed off, wiped clean, put down, set to rights. She walks back up the road.

She sits at the window of a café on the bridge over the railway line, nursing a cup of tea in her hands and looks out on to the avenue. The rain has stopped. A girl with hair the colour and texture of candy floss strides past. The three men at the table beside her are speaking in a language she doesn't understand: Eastern European, she thinks, Russian, maybe. A woman at the counter has ordered a takeaway coffee and now she is talking on her phone, explaining to the person on the other end why she is going to be late. It's because there were so many leaves still on the trees, she is saying, and they've blown off with the storm. The trains are all delayed, travelling at no more than thirty miles an hour; some of the lines have completely shut down. At this rate she'd be quicker walking to Ballymena, the woman says. She may have to take the bus. She adds 'so there are' at the end of her sentences, or 'so they have', or 'so I would', reaffirming what it is she's just said, to herself or to the person she's calling it's not clear. There's a crisis over a child who is due to be collected. Can the other person pick him up? She's sorry she's late but it's beyond her control. Everyone's late and getting later by the minute. Botanic station is like a frigging wartime evacuation, so it is; she couldn't take one more announcement about the delays; she's been standing on the platform for an hour.

Jaynie'd forgotten that people did that here, added linguistic fillers to the end of their sentences. What was that about? A lack of confidence in being believed, even when speaking the truth? For years Jaynie has lived elsewhere, in places where she has had to make herself understood, learn all the words that are acceptable, along with the words that are not. She has become *au fait* with the nuances of formal address in three different languages, of the pleasures of idiom, the pitfalls of pronunciation, how the wrong stress on a syllable can dangerously alter the meaning of a word. Her own language is thirty years out of date, fossilised in the 1980s, along with sweater dresses and faux gold. She has all the English vocabulary for tape recorders and record players, has had to learn from a distance the language of social media, of online dating, of fake news. She calculates that she has enjoyed an average of three failed relationships per continent. Would she never think of settling down, Deirdre has asked her, like it's within her gift to make such a choice, like all she has to do is decide.

She has told the principal at her current school that her brother has died, that she needed leave to come home for the funeral. She hasn't told him that between these two events is a gap of forty-seven years; that she isn't certain there will be a burial; that she hopes there will, but that she couldn't say for sure. It was too complicated to get into. She didn't want to have to explain. Hope isn't something you associate with death. It's none of their business anyway.

Had she really expected to find Botanic unchanged, to stroll into the Canterbury & Dyke and order a half dozen slices of their peppered salami? Those days in the flat on Cromwell Road when she'd grill the meat into a round of toast and sit at the Formica table in the red-carpeted kitchen with the geometric patterned wallpaper that looked like it belonged in a place where people plotted to overthrow regimes. She thought now of the fanciful fire escape mechanism over her third-floor bedroom window that had consisted of a belt and a harness and a winch that hadn't turned since God-knows-when. 'In the event of fire' she'd have taken her chances with a leap on to the bay window below. Health and safety is not what it used to be; there's that much to be thankful for. In the end, graduation became her own means of escape. 'Languages,' her mother was fond of saying, when neighbours asked what Jaynie was studying in the city. 'Sure, languages could take you anywhere.'

Outside, the wind has died down and the early evening sunlight filters through the trees. Students and uniformed schoolchildren pass, headed for the station, laden with bags and books, some still wearing their PE gear, red-legged, oblivious to the cold. And although he never went to uni, and although he'd worn his hair long, and although, if he'd lived, he'd be more than middle-aged by now, in the face of every young man that passes, in the backs of their heads, in their walk, she sees Paul.

She checks her phone. Nothing from Deirdre yet.

There's a film, a video, that's been playing in her head

now for a number of years, she's not sure how long. She stumbled on it by accident in a museum in Venice years ago, not a place she would have expected to find any trace of home. It was playing in a side gallery, in a black-painted room as she passed, when she was stalled by the sound track, a male actor's voice speaking in her own familiar accent, the unmistakeable clipped vowels, the soft northern consonants of home. In the background of the track, the sound of passing traffic, wheels on a wet road, and beyond that, birdsong. The images onscreen led her up a wet, darkening lane at twilight, bordered by shadowing hedges and barbed wire, with glimpses into green fields. She hadn't wanted to stay in the room but the voice and the images held her. The journey was haunting, mesmeric, something pale and tantalising at the lane end, something that could have been a figure, could simply have been the space where the hedges ended, a gap of light that kept changing shape. She doesn't remember all the words that were said: the mention of a body, tyre tracks, footprints, the picture of a face that was already dead. The film of the journey down the lane was spliced with other images: a close-up of a girl's face, an incident remembered, perhaps; a meeting under an underpass; a car in an abandoned lot; glimpses of alleyways, of the back end of things. She was filled, watching it, with a growing sense of dread. A car door slammed, an engine started up, tail lights glowed in the dark, the sense of a body being bundled, a kidnapping, she thought, an ambush, maybe. But she couldn't stop watching because what, or who, was that shape, dancing, at the end of the lane? And just when she thought she might make out what it was, the film returned to the point at which she had begun to watch, played through again on a loop, a circular story with no beginning or end, no real sense to it at all, and that voice again, inviting her to stay and watch and listen, to be complicit. It had winded her, momentarily, took her back to those years of growing up with images playing out on the television every night, the adults silent, grim-faced, waiting for news, always hopeful, and her hatching plans to leave.

And of course she had thought of her brother, of the last clear memory she had of him, and wondered for the thousandth time, what had happened to him.

When you are three and your brother is seventeen he stands you on his feet and walks you around the living room backwards. He rubs the puny stubble of his unshaven chin on your cheek until you squeal. When he comes in from work, he talks you into tugging off his boots and you do it, even though the boots are caked in grout and his socks stink, then out of the left one falls a brand new shiny five pence piece, the first you've ever seen. He takes the coin and rolls up his sleeves and makes it vanish into the air and plucks it out from behind your ear, with a whole bar of chocolate, untouched. When you are three, your brother is like a god to you but when you get to seventeen yourself, you know that seventeen is nothing. Seventeen is still half-child; seventeen cannot hold its drink; seventeen is riddled with mistakes. Seventeen deserves a chance to wisen up, to fill out, to brother some more; seventeen should mean being a son for longer, should mean laying the bones of your weary old parents in the ground when their time comes, and not to have them praying every night, wearing their rosary beads thin, that they will be able to do that for you. Seventeen is not a lived life. Seventeen is a heartbeat. Seventeen is waiting to begin.

He left the house to go to Fulton's to play a game of pool with Artie. Her last memory of him is of his back, of the frayed denim waistcoat he used to wear, that he'd customised himself: 'T Rex' picked out in metal studs, the biro he'd used to mark out the letters still visible around the puncture holes. All those years of wondering what had happened, of asking where he'd gone; what had been done to him; what did he do; would he ever come back?

So many questions still; more in the last few days. Did the mist cling to the hedges, Paul? Did the crows rise up as you walked? Was the ground soft and giving like it was when we used to haul home the turf? Did they lead you to the hole? Did you dig it? Did you cry? Did you say you were sorry? Did you plead with them? Did you pray? Did they hide their faces? Did they bother with masks? Did you know, early on, what that meant for you? Were you scared, Paul? Were you scared?

'Loose talk costs lives': warnings on murals everywhere. You'd said something they didn't like. Or there was something you didn't say that was expected of you, a word that was missing, or the wrong word used, maybe. Or someone misconstrued something. What was it, Paul? What coded rule did you break? Who was it that saw you, heard you, told on you, spoke out against you to save their own neck? Was it your word against theirs? Did you kiss the wrong girl? Did you whisper something in your sleep? Do they sleep, whoever they were, wherever they are now?

It is hard to think of him, if it really is him they've found, in that lonely stretch of ground for all this time. No slow drum for him; no fife playing low; no death march; no lowering down. The whistle of a weasel, maybe; or the roar of a cow, calling to her stray calves to come out of the rough ground to the sweet meadow grass. Jaynie thinks of the bog cotton swaying over him in May, the heather purpling in September. She thinks of the whooper swans, grazing through the winter, rising in April with their long necks stretched, the shape of them in the sky as they pass overhead. She thinks of the midges weaving a burr of sound under the trees in May; the smell of wild mint crushed under hooves; the pink of wild orchids in July; the trill of the curlew, the sawing of snipe.

Her phone vibrates on the table; Deirdre's name on the screen. She picks it up. There is silence and then Deirdre's voice, cracked. 'It's him, Jaynie. It's our Paul.'

Her throat makes a noise; she puts the phone down and watches until the screen goes dead. There is a pain in the centre of her forehead and she tries to concentrate on that. Outside the dark drops down like rain. In a break between buildings, the red lights of a mast rise up on Black Mountain; beneath her feet, the warning rumble of a train. The woman with the takeaway coffee is long gone, as are the men from the table beside her. Every customer that leaves the café meets their own reflection in the dark of the glass door, coming in. The street has cleared of students and schoolchildren. The lights have begun to come on.

'Cribben,' that was the word, the word they had for 'kerb'. Imagine having two words for such an inauspicious thing, for an edging, for a holding back, a restraint.

There is more than one word for the evening too but for this evening now, the word is still.

There is more than one word for the street, but this street is suddenly quiet.

There is more than one word for the shadows and these shadows are long, and lengthening.

There is more than one word for the heart but the word for her heart is sore.

# A Loss

It's hard to know what the truth of it is. I've been picking at a knot, but the looser it gets, the less I like what I see. Best to leave it as it is, maybe, though the impulse to keep worrying at it is difficult to withstand. 'The truth will out,' my aunt used to say to me as a boy, when she suspected me of keeping something from her, when I denied I'd been down to the boat slip again, begging the fishermen to take me out. As if truth were like oil and will rise to the surface; as if it will always declare itself in the end. It's the kind of idea that teachers and clerics used to terrorise us with in the past. It's the kind of idea I try to sell to my own pupils now, though we all know that they don't buy it. 'Truth is relative,' they say back to me. We're living in different times.

Aunt Sheila died September past, not long after the beginning of the new school term. She was my father's only sister. She lived just over an hour from where I live in the city, in a bungalow by the sea. She hadn't married, had taught in the grammar school in the town all of her professional life. She survived both my father and mother who passed away on the family farm, within a few months of each other, a little over a year ago. Aunt Sheila was in her late eighties and, as far as I knew, had lived in relatively good health up until a few weeks before her death when she had gone out one evening in her night clothes and suffered a fall on the sea path below her house. One of the neighbours had found her when they heard my aunt's little dog whining. I don't know what she was doing out there. I doubt that many people had seen her in her nightie before. She was a very correct sort of person, my aunt. She'd have been mortified if she'd known. As it turned out, she never regained consciousness. She'd suffered a severe contusion; must have knocked her head against the metal railing when she fell. The neighbour took the dog in at the time but wasn't keen to keep it. 'An animal's too much of a tie,' she had said.

The funeral was a quiet affair. I am my aunt's only surviving relative. A handful of uniformed school pupils, too young to have known her, formed a guard of honour at the church door; a few older parishioners, former colleagues and ex-pupils followed the cortège to the outskirts of town. She was buried in a plot she had picked out for herself in the corner of the graveyard. Afterwards, in the parish hall, over tea and a medley of sandwiches, I fielded handshakes and condolences while former pupils reminisced about their school days, told me what a dedicated teacher Aunt Sheila had been, how much she would be missed.

I hadn't visited my aunt much in recent years. My clearest memories of the place were from the seventies, the summer I was sent to stay with her. I had asthma as a child and suffered at hay-making time. My father had taken it into his head that a stay by the sea would clear my lungs. I remember sitting in the front seat of the Escort beside him, driving down the hill to her house, the first sight of the sea, the gulls wheeling, screeching overhead, the bag nets strung up along the shore, drying in the sun. My mother didn't come with us. There had always been some tension between the two women. I wonder if my mother was a little envious of what she used to call my aunt's 'independence'. The way she said it sounded pejorative, like the word she meant to use was 'selfishness'. But my father was very fond of his sister. You could see that in the way they spoke together. That visit, he brought her a bag of early spuds from the farm, a clutch of fresh eggs. 'Those'll put a bit of colour back in your cheeks,' he said.

I spent hours down at the boat slip that summer, barefooted in the shallow water, fishing in the rock pools for hermit crabs and shrimp, watching the fishermen set out to haul in the bag net, waiting for them to come back in with the catch. My aunt forbade me to go out with them, said the sea was too dangerous, unpredictable for a farm boy like me. There was one man, Bill, who used to deliver fish to her and who provided, since my aunt didn't drive, a makeshift taxi service from time to time. They were friends of sorts. I thought if I kept on at Bill, that he would relent and take me out in the boat. I used to wait for him near the ice house. He would often stop by there to pick up some fishing gear on the way out, but he wouldn't defy my aunt. 'Miss Scullion would have my guts for garters,' he used to say, and then laugh, as if he were picturing what that might look like. I remember him that summer I was there, in his flat cap, ears that stuck out like jug handles either side of his head, carrying a silver salmon up to her door. I remember Aunt Sheila in the pantry preparing the fish with a vicious-looking wooden-handled blade, slicing the scales off its back in one long strip. She was never squeamish. She'd grown up on the farm, helping my grandfather birth lambs before my father was old enough to help, before she went off to college. She didn't visit us much in the country, though Bill would drive her down now and again, and occasionally bring something for the septic tank.

The septic tank on the farm gave us trouble when it overflowed and waste from the house seeped into the lower meadow. A builder had told my father that if he dropped the carcass of a dead animal in from time to time, that it would resolve the issue. I've heard this again since: it's something to do with enzymes breaking down matter, speeding up the process of decomposition. Some people swear that it works. When the tank overflowed, my father kept a lookout for a fox or a badger killed on the road, or a stillborn lamb in the spring. The fishermen near my aunt would sometimes find dead seal cubs on the rocks in the autumn, and Bill said, if the timing was right, he would bring one down when they came. The last day they drove down to the farm, some weeks after the summer I'd spent with her, Sheila and my mother had a bit of a falling out. I remember my mother restacking the unused china after Sheila and Bill had left, clattering everything back into the cabinet in the parlour. 'Wouldn't put a foot over the threshold,' she said, 'not even for a sup of tea. The face on her. You'd think it would have poisoned her. The place where she was born. Not good enough any more for the likes of her.' I could see that the rift had saddened my father, though he didn't say much at the time. My father was a quiet man, content at his work, the round of his life dictated by the turning of the seasons, the demands of the land. When it came to a battle of words, there was no winning against my mother.

A few weeks after my aunt's funeral, during the October half term, I drove back down to the coast to sort out things at her house. As soon as my car pulled into the drive, the next-door neighbour appeared, only too glad to pass my aunt's dog back to me. 'Sheila was a good neighbour,' she said. 'She never gave us any bother, but she was getting a bit confused. Seemed to always be out on the sea path lately, looking for something she thought she'd lost. I hope she's at peace now.' I thanked her and took the dog.

It was a nervous little beast, a cross of some kind, brown and white, low-bellied, a touch of the foxhound about its face. Once inside, it sniffed around, circled its bed in the alcove beside the hearth, settled down with its chin on its paws and eyed me with suspicion. At that time I had some notion of keeping the dog. A city flat is not an ideal home for a pet, but I was thinking that at some point I might take early retirement, fix up the old farm house, settle back at home. The fields are nearly all leased out, but for a while I had a vision of myself as a gentleman farmer, strolling down to the lower meadow of a summer evening, listening out for the call of the curlew the way my father used to do, the small dog at my heels.

It was one of those dry, still days at the coast, just after the clocks go back, when it feels as if the season is holding its breath, readying itself for winter. The house was cold. I set a fire in the hearth. The place was full of furniture for which I had no use. The agents had said they'd deal with everything but I didn't want to leave any personal papers lying around—I had that much of my mother's circumspection in me, and something, I suppose, of her acquisitive nature. If she'd been alive, she would have directed me to check for any valuables that had been stashed away. The house was coming down with old schoolbooks, knitting patterns and recipes torn from magazines, novenas and relics stacked on armchairs and side tables near her bed. She'd got into the habit of jotting down anything that caught her attention off the television or the radio. On the backs of envelopes and in the margins of newspapers I found little snatches of writing in blue biro: song titles; a few lines of a prayer; the date the *Titanic* was lost; the name of a man in Sligo who had the cure for impetigo; the correct way to spatchcock a chicken. Marginalia and glosses that had importance only for her. I stuffed fistfuls of paper into bags to empty into the recycling bin. I kept a few old photos of her and Dad, one black and white snap of the two of them, dressed for Holy Communion or Confirmation, hands joined in prayer. Aunt Sheila, serious-faced, looking into the camera lens, Dad peering up, taking the cue of solemnity from her. Everything else, postcards and addressed bills, I dropped into the flames.

I was surprised to find from the agents that my aunt's estate included the ice house; she must have lent or leased it out to Bill. An old stone building, less than a quarter of a mile from the house, right on the shore facing the now disused boat slip, it was built into a lump of basalt that towered over the rear of the building. One small, high, boarded-up window looks out towards the sea. At some point a brick chimney was added to the landward side. The building was to be sold along with the bungalow. I decided to have a look to see if there was anything of interest in there.

I found the dog's lead on a hook by the back door. As soon as I picked it up the animal began to bound around the room. I locked up and headed for the steps that lead down to the sea path. The ice house is to the north, in the direction of the town, I could see its single chimney from the road, but the dog had other ideas. As soon as we emerged on to the path she tugged on the lead in the direction of the beach. I followed her, decided to leave the ice house till later. I suspected she hadn't had much exercise in the weeks before. She seemed to know where she wanted to go.

There was hardly a breath of air, the sea as flat as a mill pond, just a curl of white surf showing. The dog padded along the path and headed to a small sandy inlet just before the main strand, a spot known previously as the Gentlemen's Bathing Place. My aunt used to say that no matter what went in the water to the north, it would wash up back there. I unhooked the lead and the dog dashed down the steps to where a culverted waterway emerged from a concrete pipe, spilled over some rocks and down into the sea. She nosed around the shore, snuffling under bladderwrack and beach debris, began to tug at something that was tangled up in weed until she emerged with a pale stump, that for a split moment, I took for bone. She ran back to deposit the thing at my feet. It was a piece of driftwood, stripped of bark, light, friable, in my hand. I threw it for her and half an hour passed as I patrolled the shoreline, and the dog chased the stick in and out of the sea. Then I hooked the lead on to her collar and headed back in the direction of the ice house. As we climbed the steps from the beach back up on to the path, I felt the air grow damp and when I looked to where we were walking, I saw that a mist had begun to creep in from the sea. It was growing dark now. There are no street lights on the path, but at certain points pools of yellow light spill over from the road above. The mist thickened as I walked, diffusing the light, making it difficult to see ahead.

I was rounding a bend, not far from the ice house, when the dog stopped short and pulled to the seaward edge of the path. I couldn't see anything that would have caused her to cower. I tugged on her lead but she whimpered, refused to budge. I stepped closer to her to shorten the lead, leant for a moment against the metal railing that borders the path, and it was then that I felt a vibration, a low thrum, as if something—or someone—was knocking against it. The legs of the railing are set in the cement of the path. The dog must have felt the tremor in her feet. As I stood there, the vibration strengthened. I tugged on her lead again and a low growl grew in her. There was nothing to do but to pick her up. For a small dog, she wasn't light. Her feet and belly were wet from the sea. I took a few steps forward on the path, but as I walked towards the blind corner, she began to twist and claw at me, digging her nails into my arm, whining all the time. I swore and dropped her. The dog landed on her feet and bolted back along the way we'd come, the handle of the lead bouncing along the path behind her. I felt a damp patch on my sweater, too warm to be sea water, realised the dog had pissed on me. I retraced my steps towards the beach, calling for her, all the while cursing the fog and the dark and the damp seeping through to my skin. There was no sign of her on the small beach, or on the main strand. I walked up the path to the lights of the golf club and returned to the house by the road. When I reached it, I found the dog shivering on the doorstep.

My aunt had been teetotal, but in a cupboard in the pantry I found an unopened half bottle of whiskey, stored away, no doubt, for one of those recipes she'd collected, a Christmas cake that she never got around to baking. I helped myself to a glass or two. That night I lay in the bedroom I'd slept in on my visit as a boy, with the window on the latch, listening to the dull lap of the sea. I read for a while from one of the magazines that lay around, an uninspiring article on the benefits of walking, and then I fell asleep, unused to the narrow bed, with my knee and my hand hanging over the side. At some stage during the night, I became aware of a draught of air in the room, and I rose and closed the window, fell back into an uneasy sleep.

I woke, stiff and cramped, in the morning, with a headache and with a foul taste in my mouth, and walked into town to clear my head, leaving the dog where it was. I ate a hearty breakfast of eggs and soda bread, flicked through a newspaper, and then headed back to the house by the sea path, calling at the ice house on the way. There is only one entrance to the building, a weather-beaten door gained via a steep gravel slope to the landward side. The padlock was rusted, silted with sea air; the place had been locked up for years, but the agents must have already tried the lock, and with a bit of effort I got the key to work. It was bitter cold in there, despite the mild October weather. The walls must have been up to three feet thick in places: you couldn't hear a sound from within. The interior was brick-clad, had been used, I believe, to store fish at a time, when the shore was still used for draft netting. There was no evidence of a power supply. A hurricane lamp sat rusting by the door. Cobwebs hung in festoons from the rafters. As I stepped across the floor, something scuttled in the dark. With the light on my phone, I made out a tangle of nets, a number of discarded lobster pots, a few rusted tins of paint. And in the corner, on a mildewed, stained mattress, some tattered rags that could once have been bedding, which looked as if they hadn't been disturbed for years. Maybe someone had kept a dog or a cat in there, though the creature would have had to be let in and out since the door, as far as I remembered it, was kept locked from the outside. And it would have been a cold and a dark and a miserable bed with the high window boarded up as it had been for as long as I'd known the place. It was dry inside. That's all that could be said in its favour.

I locked up and went back to the house, relit the fire and returned to my task. My aunt, in her later years, had taken to knitting what my mother used to call 'matinée jackets' for babies: little open-weave affairs, always in pale blue, with tiny pearlised buttons and ribbons. More decorative than practical, my mother liked to say: the work of a woman who knew nothing of the messy business of motherhood. Aunt Sheila shipped them off, every now and again, to the Good Shepherds in the city. 'It's something to occupy my hands,' she would say, 'and my head.' One drawer of the chest in her bedroom was full of them. I unpacked the small garments into bags for the charity shop. I didn't have much time.

I dampened down the ashes of the fire and raked them through the grate, filled the back seat of the car with bags, put the dog and its bed in the boot and left. I pulled up at the charity shop in the town, just before it closed for the day. As I pulled the bags out of the car, a scrap of paper fell out, a few lines of something in my aunt's distinctive copperplate handwriting that could have been part of a rhyme, or a song, or something she had composed herself. I folded it into my trousers pocket and carried on with my task. Back in the flat that night, I pulled out the scrap of paper, unfolded it, and sat down on the edge of the bed to read. It was only a few words, the lines from a skipping rhyme, remembered from her childhood, or heard, perhaps, in her teaching years: 'Miss Lucy had a baby, she called him Tiny Tim. She put him in the bathtub to see if he could swim.' I'd heard the younger girls at school sing a version of the rhyme myself, but something about seeing the words in my aunt's own handwriting gave me pause. I thought again of that mattress in the ice house, of the cold and the quiet in there. And then I thought of that last day that Aunt Sheila and Bill had come to the farm, to sort out the problem with the septic tank.

The day the car arrived in the yard, we all went out to meet it. My mother said to Bill and my father to head on down to the lower meadow and she would put the kettle on. Bill hauled an old, stained sack out of the boot of the car. Aunt Sheila sat in the passenger seat and wound down the window. She said she had been a bit car sick, that she wouldn't bother coming in. My mother said a gulp of tea would do her good: 'Tell her,' she said to my father. 'You wouldn't surely drive all the way back without taking something?' But my aunt wasn't for budging. I turned my attention to Bill. I'd never seen a seal cub before.

'Was it born in the sea?' I asked him.

'What?' Bill said.

'The baby seal.'

'No,' he said. 'No, they birth on land.'

'What happened to it?' I asked.

'It's hard to say,' Bill said, and looked to my father who was talking in the car window to Aunt Sheila.

'Come on out o' that,' said my father, 'and let the man get on.'

'Can I see?' I asked Bill.

Aunt Sheila turned sharply towards me at that and, in unison with Bill and my father, said 'No.'

Bill heaved the sack on to his back.

I wanted to go with them, but my mother said the septic tank was no place for a child. I watched my father and Bill walk down the well pad towards the marshy ground, the slight weight of the sack on Bill's back, a shape in it that a small round head might make. And then my mother said that whatever about the rest of them, she wasn't going to conduct her business in the street, and she marched back to the house and called after her for me to come in. I looked at Aunt Sheila. She was paler than the last time I'd seen her, thinner too. I suppose she'd have been about forty then. She was staring after Bill and my father with a stricken look on her face, like she wished she could will them to stop with her eyes. And then my mother called me again and I had to go. I was never sent to stay with Aunt Sheila again after that.

I kept the dog in the flat for a night or two and then dropped it at an animal shelter. The neighbour was right: a dog's too much of a tie. My aunt's house was sold, the ice house along with it. I paid off the mortgage on my flat. I won't fix up the farmhouse now. I'll stay in the city where I have no history, where I can walk the streets in peace. I think of my aunt often, and wonder about her, and about the words that she wrote on that scrap of paper, words that must have been long in her head. And I marvel, not for the first time, at the secrets people keep, for themselves, and for others, at the sadnesses that betray them, and at the small quiet lives that they continue to live out until the end of their days.

# The Snagging List

Hey, Allie.
Long time no hear.
How're you doing?

> Fine. It's good to
> hear from you, Jess.
> How are things?

Good. Busy.
I heard about Stewart.
I'm really sorry.
Do you want to talk?

> No, thanks. I'm good.
> How's Majorca?

Mad busy. Can't catch a
breath. Lots of new rentals
coming on the market.

> You're still doing that?

Sure.
I have a property free
from next Saturday.
Was wondering if you
fancied a break?

> Really?

Can you get the time off?

                Maybe. Short notice but, yes.
                I think so. It'd be really good
                to see you.

About that. There's a small
catch.

                Tell me.

I won't be here.
You'd have some company,
though. A small dog named
Otso. He's a great distraction.

                I didn't know you had a dog?

He comes with the property.

                This is beginning to sound
                suspiciously like work.

Not hard work, though.
The place is amazing. It's
just been refurbed: private
pool, barbecue, all mod cons.
You'd be doing your old
friend a favour, Allie.

                What sort of dog is it?

Mixed breed. Small. Low to
the ground. All you have
to do is feed it, water it, walk
it, that's it. Give it a pat on
the head now and again, if
you're feeling affectionate.

                Is it house-trained?

Of course it's house-trained.

                OK I'm in.

Fantastic! The cleaners will
be in on Saturday. They can
let you in if you arrange a
flight for then? Just let me
know about any problems,
OK?

Where are you off to?

Somewhere deliciously cool.


*Sat 14 Sep, 15:21*


I'm here! Thank God for the
air con.

Northerner!

And thank you for the
oranges. I've never used a
juicer before. I think I might
get one.

Steady! You'll be getting
notions. I don't know why
juicers weren't more of a
thing on the estate when we
were growing up?

Don't tell anyone.

Your secret is safe with me.

Were the palm trees here
before the house?

I'm not sure. The original
house is quite old; the
kitchen's an add-on.

I counted eleven rings on one
trunk. That's if it works the
same way for palm trees as it
does for oaks.

There you go. Established,
but not ancient. Not as old as
the walls.

How old are the walls?

Middle ages.

They're sticking it well. Was
the dog always that shape?

What shape?

Long in the body; short in
the leg.

As far as I know. Is he OK?

It keeps sniffing my leg. Is
that normal?

He's building up your profile.
Has he got plenty of water?

The pool's full to the neck.

Please tell me you've given
him fresh water.
The pool water's chlorinated.

Allie?

I've given it fresh water.

Thank you!

This place is amazing. The
living area must have been
the kitchen originally? That
trough that the plants sit in

looks like an old sink. And the exposed brickwork. There must have been an open fire at one time?

There was, yes. The designer had it bricked up but kept some of the features. Very fashionable at the moment. Did you water them?

Water what?

The plants?

Oh, right. Sure thing. I will. The owners like a neutral shade, don't they? And a vessel, they're fond of a vessel, these people. What's with the fossilised pumpkin thing?

Art, my friend. It's by a local ceramicist. Very up and coming. We reckon that could be worth a bob in a year or two.

We do, do we?

Jess?

I'm here.

What's the policy on beasts?

Is there something wrong with the dog?

The dog's fine. It's pissing like a trooper against the palm

tree just now. But there's a
giant stripy buzzy thing in
the kitchen and I'm pretty
sure it's got wings.

Can you catch it in the
dustpan?

Are you mad? It's bigger than
my head!

It's probably just a hornet.
Open the window wide, it'll
find its way back out.

That would entail going
back into the kitchen. Not
happening, my friend. I've
barricaded the door. Think
I'll take a nap now. It's
astonishing how exhausting
heartache can be.

*Sat 14 Sep, 17:39*

How are you doing now?

You woke me from a
beautiful dream.

You're not in bed, are you?

Napping on the sofa. But tell
me... leather? In this heat?
Every time I turned around I
slid off like an oiled herring.

It's wipeable, though.

Practical. Use a throw?
Is the beast gone?

No idea. I'm not going back
in there again.

What'll you eat?

The pumpkin's starting to
look good.

What about Otso? You
could send him in first, like
a canary down the mine?

Who?

The dog!

Oh yeah! I don't fancy his
chances. The mouth on that
thing in the kitchen is bigger
than his. What's that noise?

What sort of noise?

There's something beeping
somewhere.

Dishwasher?

I didn't switch it on.

The fridge, maybe?

Why would the fridge beep?

Because the door's not
closed?

I definitely closed the door.
Why would it beep now?
Unless the beast has broken
in?

You're going to have to go
in there.

Nope!

OK.

Sat 14 Sep, 18:22

Damnit! The sound is
following me around the
house. It's driving me mad.
I'm going in.

I've got the net from the
pool. If you don't hear from
me, say I was brave. Say I
always saw that justice was
done. Say I spoke up for the
downtrodden, for the weak,
for those with no voice.
Jess?
Pray for me?

What was it?

The fridge door wasn't shut.

Any sign of the beast?

No. I'm hoping it got out.
I've locked all the windows
and doors.

That's good.

I'm not sure. It looked like it
might have its own key.

What does yer woman next door have to talk about outside in the street until all hours of the night? She was right under my window till after midnight, giving it welly.

*Your* window?

You know what I mean. I thought someone had left on a radio. She never stops to draw breath. I wish I knew what the hell she was saying.

She's probably discussing the odd one renting the house next door.

Badda boom!

The street's her garden, essentially. She's the local entertainment.

She's knitting something, I think, or sewing, clacking away on those wooden bobbin things. Plus, she thinks I should cover up.

How do you know?

Lots of pointing when I was out earlier, at the sun, at my bare shoulders. '*Blanca, blanca;*

*el sol, el sol!'*

Your Spanish is coming on.

Thanks. She's keeping an eye
on me. The dog had a huge
crap outside her front door
and she was out before I got
the bag out of my pocket.

Glad to hear you're cleaning
up after him.

I don't have much choice.
Are the light switches meant to
be some kind of intelligence
test? I dropped a tin of lip
salve out of bed last night and
all the lights came on in the
bedroom. I didn't even know
there was a switch on the
floor. It put the life out of me.

It'll take a bit of getting
used to.

And while we're at it, why's
there no door on the ensuite?
Is that a continental thing?
No one, no matter how close
they are to me, wants to hear
my digestive system evacuate
in the morning.

I'm beginning to have
some sympathy for Stewart.

Too soon?

Too soon.

Apologies.
The door's been ordered.
There's been some delay.

I'm taking it in turns to test
all the toilets. My favourite is
the one downstairs, beside the
kitchen. By the way, they'll
have to provide more loo roll
for guests.

Ease off on the oranges,
maybe?

You could have a point.
How's Finland?

Very cool.


*Mon 16 Sep, 20:03*


The mossies are having a
field day feasting on me. Ten
bites and counting, all of
them infected. The citronella
burner is officially rubbish at
keeping them away.

Officially laughing out loud.
How's Otso?

Who?

Are we still doing this?
The dog!

He's fine. Absolutely no use

against the mossies. Is there some kind of narcotic in those yellow flowers that grow high up in the palms? The wasps spend the entire day at them, and when they come down, they're totally chilled and silent, nothing like those vicious buzzy bastards we have at home.

They say that insects take on national characteristics.

What are the Finnish wasps like?

Efficient. Respectful. They only buzz when it's absolutely required.

Nice. They're mad for those little flowers. The courtyard's covered in the husks. I thought it was sawdust at first. Who's LK?

Why do you ask?

The outside wall of the kitchen extension. There's a pattern that looks like moons rising, or suns setting, behind a series of hills. The initials are inscribed in the mortar.

I hadn't noticed that.

The plasterer must have

fancied himself as a bit of an
artist.

What the hell?
It's raining! You never said
anything about rain.

I have no dominion over
the skies. Did you bring the
cushions in from the lounger?

Allie?

I have now.
What's that smell?

Enlighten me.

In the kitchen.
It smells of sewer.

It could be the drains.
Try running some water.

That's done the trick.

No sign of the giant winged
beast?

Crap! I forgot all about it.
I'm hiding out in the living
room now.

What's with the rust effect on
all those metal shelving units
and cupboard doors in here?
Is this stuff recycled?

It's Corten steel. Ready-
weathered, for the industrial

look. The new contrasting
with the old. It's quite
expensive.

It's quite impractical. It stains
very badly.

What did you spill?

Never mind.

You're not drinking, Allie?

Allie?

You know that's not a good
idea.

I'm down to half a litre of
mosquito repellent a day.

No alcohol. You know it
doesn't help.


*Tue 17 Sep, 20:17*

Fernando's seafood paella is
the business!

You still avoiding the
kitchen?

Uh huh.

Did he try to chat you up?

He said I had skin like
porcelain.

The light is kind in the south.
Did you show him your

mossie bites?

>     Too soon for jokes about my
>     war wounds, my friend.

>     Was the interior designer tall,
>     by any chance?

Interesting question. Why do
you ask?

>     I was slapping on some
>     make-up before I came out.
>     I had an excellent view in
>     the ensuite mirror of my face
>     from the nostrils up.

Short-arse!

>     I'm five foot five, same as
>     you. Plus, that third setting
>     in the shower? The shoulder
>     massage? The water jet hit me
>     square in the eye.

I'll pass that on.

>     The dark comes down early,
>     doesn't it?

It does. Are you OK?

>     Yeah. I'm fine.

There are some DVDs in the
house, if you fancy watching
a film?

>     DVDs. There's nostalgia. I'll
>     have a look when I get back.

What about Fernando?

>     He's chatting to a redhead.

She's cracking a pair of
lobster legs at him like they're
maracas. I think he's over me.

*Tue 17 Sep, 22:31*

My my! Pierce is no
Benny or Björn, is he?

*Mamma Mia?*

Here I go again.

My My!

How can I resist ya?

Still, it passed the time. And
took my mind off the scene
of carnage in the downstairs
toilet.

Fernando's seafood paella?

Dead giant winged thing.

The beast?

The beast. It must have been
lurking behind the toilet
bowl. It waited till I got
settled on the loo then it rose
up like the angel of death. I
nearly lost the run of myself.
Got it with the toilet brush
in the end. The cleaners may
need extra this week.

Please don't tell me any more.

I thought I heard it in here

earlier.  A sinister fluttering.
It turned out to be that plastic
bag they've put over the
disused flue where the hearth
used to be? It sucks air in and
out with the breeze. Like an
asthmatic Darth Vader. Or a
trapped bird.

I'd forgotten about that. I'll
make a note. Cheers, Missus.
You're doing a great job.

Between that and the jabber
of yer woman next door, it's
like Piccadilly Circus in here.

She's outside my brief, I'm
afraid.

I hope you get some sleep
tonight.

Me too. Night, Jess.

Night, Allie.


*Wed 18 Sep, 16:35*

Jess?

Allie.

The wee man with the horns
and the tight grip on the
blackthorn stick?

Neighbour to the other side?

Ye're a geg! Sculpture, in the living room, about two feet tall? I've put him behind the TV cabinet, if the owners are looking for him. He's giving me the heebie-jeebies, him and his big high-stepping leg.

Ha! Noted. Anything else?

I take it you're not letting to families with children?

Why do you say that?

That second bedroom upstairs, with the two single beds?

Yes?

The balustrading on the windows isn't high enough. A child could easily climb it. Accident waiting to happen.

D'you reckon?

Absolutely. Plus the pool's too deep for kids. The water comes up over my head.

Even on tiptoe?

Yes, sirree. 'Not child friendly.' Put that in the brochure.

You're well informed for a barren old spinster. No offence, like.

I'm the same age as you! It's

those squads of nieces and
nephews I've minded over
the years. I'm like blooming
Nanny McPhee.

How many strokes did you
manage in the pool?

Three, before I sank. It's
hardly Olympic size, is it?

It's just a plunge pool,
designed to cool you off.

Or to drown you, if you're
not six feet tall. I can't
remember the last time I
went swimming. Do you
remember learning, at the
Protestant school?

Ha! You've made me spill my
tea! It's years since I thought
of that.

Tea? You've mended your
ways. She was a witch, that
swimming instructor. She
chucked me in the deep
end. Do you think she only
did that to the Catholic
schoolchildren?

You're a hoot! You think she
could tell to look at us?

She could tell by the name of
the visiting school. She nearly
drowned me twice. Speaking

of schooldays, have you
noticed the portrait of Sister
Immaculata in the porch at
the church in the square?
Same expression exactly:
'Move an inch and I'll bite
your nose off, girl.'

I suppose she could have
had Majorcan relations.
What were you doing in the
church?

I followed the sound of bells.
There are three different sets,
have you noticed?  And they
ring two minutes apart. Not
great for time-keeping.

You're on holiday. Time is
meaningless. Was the church
worth a visit?

You haven't been?

Not for about fifteen years.

Dark, oppressive,
disappointing.

Disappointing? How?

They've got those battery-
operated candles. No naked
flame to dispel the gloom.

Did you say a prayer?

I sent up some thoughts.

I hope they land where you
want them to.

Allie?

Yeah?

I always thought you were
too good for him.

That's meant to be a comfort,
I suppose? You don't know
the whole story.

Was there someone else?

No. I don't think so, though
I don't reckon Stewart will be
single for long. He's not good
at being on his own.

We were trying, you know?

You certainly could be.

For a baby. We were trying
for a baby.

I didn't realise.

No one knew. I'm not sure
Stewart was all that keen. It
was me who was driving it.
Ticking clock and all that.

I'm sorry, Allie.

I got pregnant. Twice.

Why didn't you say?

You know. The usual caution,
bred into us. Bordering on
superstition. 'Wait until after
the first twelve weeks before
you say anything.' Just as

well, really. We nearly made
it to twelve the last time.
And then, I don't know, after
that, we just couldn't make it
happen again.

I don't know what to say,
Allie. I'm so sorry.

I don't think Stewart could
have gone through it again.
Could have dealt with me
going through it again. It sort
of broke us.

I'll phone you.

No, it's OK. I'm fine. This is
easier, somehow. Beating it
out like this.

Are you sure?

Yeah. It's just that, I've lost
more than him, you know?


*Thu 19 Sep, 12:19*

That's the obligatory trip to
the beach over and done with.

Not your scene?

Not enough shade for this
lump of scarified flesh.

Did you go in for a swim?

A quick dip. I got the shock
of my life. The water was

65

warm. Not a single intake of breath.

The courtyard here doesn't get much sun, does it? It's almost entirely in the shade by five.

That's the idea. To keep the house cool.

Don't tourists come for a suntan?

They can get a tan on the beach. The house is designed to be more of a sanctuary, a retreat. 'Casa Calma', you know?

Get you! Sanctuary, indeed! Far from a calm house were you reared!

Did you remember to feed the dog?

Of course I remembered to feed the dog. He follows me around, whinging, until I do. The plants would fare better if they had legs. And a voice box. How's Finland?

Good.

And the man?

What man?

Come on, Jess. You've never

mentioned Finland before and I know your company doesn't have rentals there. I checked. What other reason could there be?

Rumbled.

Yep. Are you going to tell me about him?

Well, he's Finnish.

Name?

Leo.

Uh huh?

Leo Kemppainen.

Have you met his family?

Yes. They're lovely. Very chilled.

Ha! Chilled! In Finland! What does he do?

Jess?

Are you there?

It wasn't that bad a joke.

He's a very tall designer.

Seriously?

Seriously.

The mysterious LK.

I'm sorry. I should have said. Only, it's early days.

Early days? You're in Finland,

meeting his family. Sounds
pretty serious to me.

I know. It's just that things
have moved quickly. And I
didn't want to go on about
him, what with you and
Stewart and everything.

I'm not that fragile, Jess. I'm
happy for you. Are you going
to move in together?

That's the plan.

Allie?

Yeah?

I'm pregnant.

Allie?

Wow! Just wow! I don't know
what to say. Congratulations!
That's really good news.

Thank you.
I'm sorry.
This is not what you want to
hear right now.

Don't apologise because
things are working out for
you, Jess. Misery doesn't
always need company. Misery
can be miserable all on its
own. So you're going to try
to make a go of it?

It looks like it.

> Good for you. I'm glad.
> Honestly. I'm happy for you
> both.

*Fri 20 Sep, 17:29*

> That grey rendered wall,
> at the back of the pool,
> Jess? It must be thirty feet
> high. When the sun hits
> it in the evenings, it's like
> a giant projection screen.
> The shadow of the palms is
> cast against it, as well as the
> shadows of all the visitors,
> walking along the ramparts.
> I see their outlines before I
> hear them. They move across
> it like ghosts. They don't
> realise there's anyone here,
> that I can hear them. The
> courtyard walls are too high.
> All those stories, all those
> lives, disembodied, at one
> remove from themselves.

> Are you there, Jess?

I'm here, Allie.

> How far on are you?

As of today, thirteen weeks.

> That's good. And you're
> keeping well?

So far, yes. A bit nauseous on
the plane on the way out.

> That's a good sign, they say.

Is it?

> Yeah.

That's good.

> This is his house, isn't it,
> your tall designer's?

It is.

> And you're going to live here,
> together?

We are.

> You hadn't planned for this,
> for the baby?

No. The house was meant to
be an investment. A rental.
We're going to have to make
a few changes. Thanks for the
snagging list.

> Don't mention it.

Are you all set for the airport
tomorrow?

> All sorted.

> Were you fond of those plants
> in the old sink?

Why the past tense?

> They haven't done so well in

the heat.

Did they ever see water?

Not on my watch.

At least the dog has survived.
The dog *is* alive?

Allie?

Just been to check. He looks fine.

I think I might get one.

A dog? Really?

A plant. I reckon it'd be a good idea to start small in the nurturing stakes, see how that goes. Plus, it'd be good company.

You are still talking about a plant?

Yeah. I mean, not company, exactly, but you know, a focus. Something to look after, something to come home to.

You do know how sad that sounds?

Yeah. Maybe you're right. Maybe it's too soon.
Yer woman next door, bobbins going in time with her mouth. Does she know?

Know what?

                About the baby?

No. Of course not. I haven't
told anyone. We wanted to
talk to Leo's family first. Why
do you ask?

                She must be some kind of
                seer. She gave me something
                today. A little square of white
                lace. I've left it for you on the
                sideboard, beside the petrified
                pumpkin. It'd be perfect for a
                christening bonnet, if you're
                still into that kind of thing?

Thank you, Allie.
You'll come back? When
we're all settled. I'd like you
to meet Leo. And this little
person, whoever they turn
out to be, is going to need a
godmother.

                Really?

Really.

                Are you sure?
                I killed the plants.

Otso survived.

                You're absolutely sure he's
                always been that shape?

Stop it! Will you do it?

                I'd love to. Just get that
                snagging list sorted, OK?

This place is not child-ready.

We will.

Allie?

I'm here.

You're going to be OK.

I know. Thanks, Jess, for the
loan of the house.
It's been good.

You're welcome.

Safe home, my friend.

You too. x

# The Escapologist

There is a boy in my room, a stranger, a boy with dark wet hair. He's sitting on the edge of the bed rubbing the back of his neck. He is dripping water over the duvet cover. There's a damp patch where he is.

I don't know how he got in. I keep my room locked when I leave the house. The window is always fastened. It is a small room, on the third floor. The window opens on to the street. It's not raining outside. I have a divan bed. There's no room underneath for a boy to hide, not even a smallish one such as this. Before I left, I opened the wardrobe to pull out a jacket. I'd have noticed if he'd been in there. I've only been gone for a few minutes, turned at the bottom of the stairs to fetch a library book I need to return. It's not like me to forget things. The barrage of project deadlines must be taking its toll.

I sort through the jumble of questions in my head to choose which one to ask. 'Who are you?' seems pressing, although, on consideration, how much does that matter in the great scheme of things? 'How did you get in?' A satisfactory answer would solve the riddle, but not help me with his purpose here. I can see that he is in a state of confusion, is looking up at me with some consternation on his face. I can also see now that the initial surprise of finding him there has subsided a little, that his shirt, pale blue, frayed at the collar, is sticking, wet, to his thin shoulders and arms. His trousers, dark, belt-looped, school issue, are dripping water on to the rag rug to the side of the bed. He could be ten, eleven, maybe. In the event, it is he who speaks first. 'Who are you?' he says.

There is something familiar about him, the snaggle tooth, the freckled nose, a parting in his hair where a parting shouldn't be, a strip of pale scalp exposed. 'I'm Callie,' I tell him. 'I live here. This—' I motion, 'This is my room.'

He looks around. There's not much to see. I keep the place tidy, the way I've been taught. Everything here is rented, pre-used. You don't want to ever get too attached. You never know when you'll have to pack up and leave with little notice. If I had to, I could fit all I need into one good-sized plastic bag.

'How did I come to be here?' he asks.

So he's the one with the questions. I must admit to feeling a little defensive. 'I was about to ask you that. I'm on my way to class. I forgot my book.' I point to the title on my desk: 'It's due back to the library today.'

'I see,' he says, and looks at the book: *Predictive Modelling*. He says, 'Yes, you don't want to get a fine.'

'Are you staying?' I ask.

He looks at me. 'I'm not sure,' he says.

'I have to go.' He looks concerned. 'I'll lock the door. You'll be safe in here. See you when I get back?'

He nods, looks down at his bare wet feet. The hem of his left trouser leg has unravelled. On the rug: a padlock, a coil of chain. 'There are clothes in the wardrobe,' I tell him. 'You can change into something dry, if you like.'

I go to class but I'm a little distracted. 'S is for space; t is for time,' but the equations resist solution; schematics withhold their usual charm. When I return I go straight up the stairs. The boy is still there; he is under the duvet. He is wearing the Aran sweater that Granny June knitted. 'I make no difference,' she liked to say, needles clicking, pattern growing. 'Fostered or not, I treat them all the same.' The sweater is too big for the boy. In its folds he is small and pale. The colour washes him out.

'Are you hungry?' I ask him. He nods. 'Do you like macaroni cheese?'

'Maybe.'

'It's all I have.'

'Yes,' he says.

The kitchen is empty when I go down. I take the leftovers from the fridge and reheat them in the microwave. I stack two platefuls on my tray, two forks, climb back up the stairs. We eat together, in silence, he under the duvet, me on the side of the bed. It's how I usually eat the evening meal. When we're done, I bring the dishes down and wash them, put everything away. Then I pour two glasses of water from the tap. The student who lives on the floor below comes in. We were alone in the house the first week of the new semester when he shared his bottle of supermarket vodka with me. Now he looks at the glasses in my hand. 'You got company?' he asks.

I shake my head. 'Thirsty,' I say. I go back upstairs to my room.

The boy in my room has more questions: the name of

the city, the date, the year? He nods when I answer and asks for pencil and paper. He draws line graphs, calculations, formulae I've never seen before. He seems to be counting back in time. He rubs the back of his neck again.

I have to go out so I give him the room key. 'The bathroom is across the hall,' I say. 'Try to go when the house is quiet. No one else knows you're here.'

I meet my mother in the library café, my natural mother, the unnatural one. She smells of cigarettes and damp hallways. Her hair is stringy, unwashed. She complains about the three bus rides across town, about the price they charge for a cup of tea in this part of the city. But I like it here in the library, with the weight of the books overhead, and the solid red brick at my back, and the pink cherry blossom in bloom through the tinted glass. She asks how it's going. I say it goes well. 'You're as white as a sheet,' she says. 'Too much studying. I don't know how you stick it here.' She asks me for money. I say I have none to spare so she goes away again.

In the flowerbeds in the park there are hyacinths growing as if anything is possible. Their blue star fragrance follows me the whole way back.

When night comes down the boy curls up, lies with his face to the window. I climb into the narrow bed at his back, curl my knees under his.

'How would it be if I stayed?' he asks.

I look around the room. 'There's not enough space,' I say. His body tenses. He pulls his knees up tight to his hollow chest.

The boy asks if I can get him some things. He needs wood, he says, nails and glue, a hammer, a saw, hasps and hinges, a second padlock, a lock pick, if I can get them. He doesn't have any money. In the street behind, they are gutting a house; broken floorboards pile up in the skip outside. The builders have taken no care in wrenching them up. The boards have jagged, splintered edges. I bring them back, a few at a time. On the stairs I meet the student again, the one from the floor below. He nods at the planks of wood. A smile tugs at the corner of his mouth: 'Good idea,' he says. 'The springs on that mattress of yours are lethal. I might do the same with my own.'

The boy in my room looks at the wood, says, 'Tongue-and-groove. That's good. Watertight.' I stack the boards beside the bed, catch a splinter in my thumb. It buries itself too deep to pry out. I buy him the other things from the hardware shop over the river. I ask him to work when the house is empty. He says he'll listen for the sound of the front door.

He builds a crate with a watertight lid. He fits exactly inside. He asks if I will help him. I say I will do what I can. He shows me how to coil the chains around him, how to make the padlock fast. He shows me how to lock the crate. He looks at the two empty glasses on the bedside table. 'We will need a lot of water,' he says.

I go back to the hardware store and buy a yellow bucket. The colour matches exactly my favourite bobble hat. I meet the student again as I'm coming through the front door. He eyes the bucket, eyes my hat, raises an eyebrow at me, but he doesn't ask me anything. He is already moving away, looking down, thumbing a message into his phone.

I skip a class. We wait until we're sure the house is empty. I fill the bucket from the shower across the hall. 'Lukewarm, please,' the boy in my room says. I empty bucketfuls of water into the crate until it is three quarters full. 'We'll only have one chance at this,' he says.

He climbs into the crate. I chain him as instructed, place the lock pick between his hands. He has cut a round hole in the lid, big enough to reach through. He says, 'Thank you, Callie. Goodbye,' and takes a deep breath, and then a second, empties his lungs after each. Then he takes a third breath and closes his eyes and ducks under the water and stays. I shut the lid, fasten the padlock, go out and lock the door.

It takes days to dry out the room afterwards. I mop up the floor, return the broken planks to the skip, store the hammer and padlock in the bottom of the wardrobe. The student downstairs asks to borrow the bucket, complains to the landlord about a leak in the ceiling. After a while he moves out, says he can't concentrate with the constant hammering, can't stand the racket the builders are making in the street behind. I go to class and come home again, eat in my room, sleep in my bed. It's a good size of a room for one person, I think. It has everything I need. I can still feel the splinter, under my skin, but you can't see now where it entered the flesh. Sometimes at night I think I hear the rattle of a padlock. Sometimes in the morning, I see damp footprints on the boards of the floor where the rag rug will not reach.

# Glass Girl

There is something wrong with my sister, Evangeline. She is thin and light for a ten-year-old, and her toes turn in when she walks. She carries the wrist of one hand in the other, as if it is not a part of her, as if she is taking care of it for someone else. Her elbows stick out either side of her body and her ears stick out either side of her head. Her fingers and toes are long and bony, her legs look like they are not fit to support her, could not be capable of lifting and moving the thick-soled black shoes she needs to wear, that fix her to the ground like weights. Her pale green eyes are over-sensitive to light. She has a sensation, she says, from time to time, of something feathery brushing over her skin. I find it hard to shake the idea that my sister is a creature tethered to the earth that was originally designed for flight.

The doctors have said that Evangeline needs to strengthen the muscles of her legs, that walking on sand in bare feet is good for this. With sand, they say, there is the correct balance of support and give. This does not sound like a medical treatment to me, but every dry day since I have come to the coast to stay with my father, I have taken my sister to walk on the strand. We set out from the house and make our way along the cliff path past the smell of salt and drying seaweed and down the graffitied concrete steps that lead to the beach.

My father is Evangeline's father, and Catherine is her mother. My mother is dead. Evangeline is my half-sister, but I won't say 'half' about Evangeline. She is completely whole to me. Ours is a complicated story but that is just the way of things.

Evangeline knows the names of all the wild flowers and on our walk she tries to teach them to me: birdsfoot trefoil, marsh marigold, forget-me-nots, wild thyme. She won't allow me to pick them to use them in my work. She says they are where they ought to be and I must learn to leave them alone. If the tide is out when we reach the strand head, we take off our shoes and go searching in the rock pools for shrimp and limpets and hermit crabs and I photograph them for her. This is the only form of capture she will allow. If the tide is in, we climb into the dunes and lie on our backs with the roar of the sea behind us and listen for the rattle of magpies and make shapes out of the clouds overhead.

On the days when it's too wet to walk to the beach, when the rain bounces off the tarmac on the road and drums a steady rhythm on the roof of the house, Evangeline sits, cross-legged on the living room floor with her headphones pinning flat her ears and cuts photographs out of magazines and sticks them into scrapbooks. Mostly, these are pictures of plants and flowers and sea life and she asks me to pronounce the names for her and repeats them over and over until she has memorised every one. At night when she asks for a story, I tell her one of my mother's, the ones that she used to carry about in her head, that she got from her mother and grandmother; legends of treasure sunken in moss holes, of children stolen by fairies, stories from the island.

'You're so good with Evangeline,' Catherine says, but the truth is that Evangeline is good with me. Since my mother's funeral, the world has been blurred at the edges, altered in a way I can't explain. I am unsure, when I speak, of the right order of words. My voice sounds overloud in my head. I cannot find the language to talk to my father.

'You've had a shock,' Catherine says. 'It will take time to get over it.' But Evangeline seems to understand, Evangeline who said when I came here: 'Don't worry, my Ella, we'll look after you now.'

Today, Evangeline has an appointment at the hospital and I have the day to myself. 'Take the bike,' Catherine says. 'See a bit of the coast.'

Outside, my father unclamps the child's seat from behind the saddle of the old yellow bicycle, pumps up the tyres, says, 'Good as new. But I could drop you somewhere, pick you up, if you want?' He looks to the west, to the grey bank of mist that has hung for hours over the Barmouth, the flattened stretch of water beginning to silver and stir in the bay, a trace of damp in the air. I toy with the raindrop of green glass in my pocket, polish it under my thumb, check that the key is still attached. I remember the soft orange bulb the glass made in the gas flame when I worked it, the molten possibilities of it before it hardened and cooled. And still I cannot speak to him.

'There's a mist coming in,' my father says, not looking at me.

Evangeline trips out of the house, followed by Catherine, takes hold of my father's hand and lowers herself into the bicycle seat balanced on the ground. She sits in the seat with her bony knees up either side of her ears, intent on braiding the safety straps. Without looking up she says, 'Bring me back a picture, my Ella.' I reach down, run the dark ponytail of her hair through my hand.

'We won't be long,' my father is saying. 'I'll phone you when we're done.' My phone is in my raincoat pocket. I don't tell him that I've switched it off.

'Will you cross to the island?' says Catherine.

He shoots her a look of alarm. 'It's too far, surely?' he says. He avoids all talk of my mother, as if mentioning her will crack me in two. And I can tell that he's still angry with me, about Liam, about everything that happened.

'I'll see how I go,' I say to Catherine, and heft my rucksack on my back and straddle the bike, and blow a kiss to Evangeline. When I push off all three of them wave to me from the drive of the house.

It feels strange to cycle away without Evangeline's thin arms around my middle, without the slight weight and wobble of her in the seat behind. All summer we've toured the cycle paths, into the swimming pool in town for her water exercises, over to the amusements in Portrush where she is transfixed by the 2p machines. 'Just one more, my Ella,' she says each time we drop a coin through the slot, and she holds her breath as the tray sweeps forward, and squeals at the anticipated cascade of metal into the scoop below.

It's the tail end of August and already the colours are

84

starting to turn. I follow the tourist route, past the golf links and rows of caravans that nose the road around the coast. At Dunluce the limestone is streaked with the green and black of old watercourses; a marker in the sea beyond the ruined castle surfaces like the spire of a drowned church. Beyond Dunseverick I have to dismount when the climb proves too much for the old bike's gears, my thighs beginning to ache. At Portnareevy the sun breaks through and I pull into the viewing point. Across the water I can just see the chalk cliffs of the island picked out in the sun, green uplands above, the dark hollow of the bay, the northern side cloaked in mist. It's too far for me to see the tower of the church, the crooked white headstones where my mother is buried along with her mother and father. I take my camera from the rucksack, aim it at the white tip of the lighthouse in the east, the blue peak of Kintyre beyond.

My father moved here when he married Catherine, a year or two before Evangeline was born, but until this summer, I've only ever spent weekends here. When I was younger, he travelled to see me in Belfast, fitted visits in around site meetings and client appointments, collected and dropped me at the door. After he left, my mother and father spoke rarely. They texted when they needed to make arrangements about me. When he asked after her, I said she was fine. I am guilty, I know, of years of deceit, of the show I kept up to hide her drinking from him, from everyone. We were a good team. She went out to work every weekday; I never missed a day at school. Monday to Friday she was a model citizen. She'd wave me off on Saturday morning and be nearly sober when I got home on Sunday night. By the time my father figured things out I was old enough to choose where to live for myself.

'You have to leave, Ella,' he said. 'You're not responsible for her. You have to think of yourself.'

'Like you did?' I said and that ended the discussion. That was unfair, I know. She didn't drink when he lived with us. It had gotten worse over the years. The truth is, it was easier for me to stay and to worry than it was to worry and go. At least if I was there, I thought, I could keep an eye on her, monitor the level of intake. In the end I failed even to do that.

My father bought me this camera for my twenty-first birthday, turned up at the glass workshop in the college on the day, too tall and tidy in his suit. It had been weeks since I'd seen him, since the last argument about my mother, about what should be done. I'd stopped answering his calls. He walked in at the point when Liam had been helping me remove some pieces from the annealing oven. Liam moved away too quickly when my father appeared, busied himself with another group of students. I saw my father note it. I did not introduce them.

'Where have you been?' he said.

'Here,' I said. 'Working.' He glanced at Liam. He didn't seem to like what he saw.

'I've booked us a table,' he said, 'for tonight.' I didn't speak. 'That is, if you're free?'

'I'm not.'

'Tomorrow then?'

'You're not supposed to be in here,' I said, running my hands over the glass pieces, checking for fissures, for flaws.

'Okay,' he said. 'If that's the way you want it. Happy Birthday, Ella,' and he slid a gift bag under the workbench and left.

I couldn't believe it when I saw the camera; I hadn't known how much I'd wanted one. I was sorry I'd been hard on him. It wasn't all his fault; most of it was my mother's, I knew that. It was just easier to blame him since he wasn't there.

He has been talking lately about my plans for the future. He says there's a job in his office, junior draughtsperson; he could teach me the ropes.

'Give her some time,' Catherine says when he starts to talk about this, but time is not going to make his offer any more attractive to me. We have had to let the Belfast house go. The landlord found a new tenant; all my materials are packed into boxes in my father's house. But as I look out from Portnareevy, I am thinking of a shingle shore and a bay of purple kelp; of a gravel path by a dry-stone wall overgrown with fuchsia. I am thinking of a red tin roof and a whitewashed chimney. I am thinking of a gable that is rendered with shells and rounded pieces of bottle glass, brown and blue, that glint when they catch the sun. I am thinking of a blackened hearth and the smell of old soot and a byre that could be a workshop: my mother's home on the island.

When I first tried my hand at glass-making, I was mesmerised by the process, the movement of the glass rod in the flame, the change in the colour through blue, white, yellow, green. The rod that, moments earlier, would have shattered had it been dropped on the ground became a molten rope that could be manipulated, balled, drawn out thin as a thread. I learned how to blow glass tubing until it ballooned into a globe; learned how to turn and shape it in the flame, hollow it out with a knife. I watched, entranced, as gravity did the work of modeller. I pinched the ends with tweezers, nipped off the unwanted stalk, my favourite part, closing off the glass. I attempted snow globes but as I experimented, the glass vessels grew narrower so that they began to resemble not made but grown things. After that, nothing I created had a base. None of my work stood up by itself.

Liam became my tutor in final year. When he saw what I'd made, he directed me towards the work of Stankard. I studied the flame worker's exquisite paperweights: lifelike glass honeycombs with hovering bees; pink-petalled tea roses complete with stamen; haws and blueberries, their stems intact. But I was surprised to find that in his work there was too much artifice for me. I did not want the solid. Weight was the opposite of what I was striving for.

'There is no point in making a thing,' Liam said to us, 'if there is no emotional risk to it. You need to be prepared to make yourself fragile. You need to be afraid to expose some breakable part of yourself.' I knew he was married but when he said that I didn't care. I'd have risked anything to have him.

I began to use the glass as a thin-walled cell to house the things I found. In one elongated piece I inserted a dried mimosa bud, fused the organic stem into the closure with a molten string of glass. In another I placed a pine cone, then a chestnut burr, a dead beetle, a dried moth from my windowsill. My heart fluttered when I reheated and squeezed the openings shut, attaching glass tendrils, colouring the glass, until it was impossible to tell where the natural ended and the made began. The pieces I created for my final exhibition I had to suspend by wires from a frame. They looked like unopened shells, seedpods, egg sacs, discarded skins.

'What are they for?' my father said the night of the final exhibition. I wanted to say that 'use' didn't come into it, but I knew what his response would be to that. I don't know how to tell him that this is something I need to do; that it may help me to find what I can no longer find in language, that finding it might make the world bearable again.

'They're beautiful,' Catherine said when she saw them. 'They look like they've grown there. Like they were meant to be.'

'They're sad,' Evangeline said. 'Why are they sad?'

'How do you know stuff?' I said to her, taking her small hand.

'I see through you, my Ella,' she said.

My mother didn't make it to the exhibition opening. 'It's there for a few weeks, isn't it darling? I'll go when it's quieter, when I can take it all in.' She'd started drinking before I left the house.

After the reception, when the guests had all gone, Liam

joined the final year students in the pub. He stayed apart from me most of the night but I was aware of his every move, the lowering of his mouth to the glass when he drank, his hand reaching for the phone in his back pocket, his eyes on me when I rose. I knew where this was headed. I could afford to wait. The others drifted off, some to a nightclub, some to another bar. Liam's flat was a ten-minute walk away. 'I've got it to myself tonight,' he said.

His work was scattered on high shelves throughout the rooms, bizarrely shaped glass objects, comic strip characters welded to glass lava, experimental forms. We kissed on the living room sofa, abandoned our coffee cups and climbed the carpeted stairs. It was hard not to feel a pang of guilt at the toys strewn around the living room, the small pile of shoes inside the front door. In the bedroom he took a towel from a linen basket, laid it out on the quilt over the bed. There wasn't much spontaneity about it: the sex, through a fug of beer and shots, was joyless in the end. In the kitchen afterwards, pouring myself a glass of water, I uncurled the dog-eared corner of a crayoned drawing taped to the fridge door.

'Don't touch anything,' Liam said from behind me and slipped his arms around my waist. 'Come back to bed.' I stayed the night; thought I'd give my mother something to worry about, supposing she was conscious enough for that. In the morning Liam woke me, said he was sorry: I'd have to leave; he wasn't sure what time his wife would be back.

I walked through the city in the thin light before the buses had begun to run, past the still-shuttered shops and the littered pavements, the spoils of the night before. In the doorway of a bank on Donegall Square, a girl curled into a sleeping bag, a polystyrene food container at her head. I followed the street sweepers brushing the kerbs from City Hall up to Bradbury Place. On Botanic, a train rumbled under the road. I turned into our own car-lined street, twisted the key in the lock of the front door: my mother's heeled shoes in the hall, her bag on the ground beside them. I climbed the stairs, headed for my bedroom, but the door to her room was open, the smell of stale alcohol seeping out, the smell of vomit too. I pushed the door wide. She was lying, face-down on a dried pool of sick on top of the bed, still wearing the spaghetti-strap dress from the night before, open-mouthed, shut-eyed, blue-tinged, cold to the touch.

At Portnareevy I take the phone out of my pocket and switch it on. There are three missed calls from my father and a text that reads, 'Whereabouts are you? We'll pick you up?' I slip the phone back into my pocket. As I climb back on the bicycle, I see a white line stretch across the grey water: the wake of the car ferry crossing the Sound, almost at the mainland now. I have twenty minutes to make the harbour.

From here, the journey is easier; I can feel the gradual descent into the ferry town. The road winds through conifers. Past the slender trunks of the trees I can see the boat nearing the shore: glimpses of the vehicles on board, the mist closing in behind. The air dampens. Further on I hear the rattle of chains as the boat moors, the scrape of metal on concrete when the ridged ramp is lowered on to the quay, the sound of engines moving off. I freewheel down the steep hill towards the town.

I am rounding a bend on the sloping road when a white pick-up truck speeds towards me, a guy at the wheel in a baseball cap, music blaring from the wound-down window. I brake and put my feet to the ground, pull in to the verge but as it passes, the truck hits a pothole, there is a rattle in the back, a jolt towards the tailgate, and the gate bursts open, landing two wooden crates with a crash on the tarmac a few feet behind me. I turn in the saddle to shout after the driver but he is hurtling along oblivious to what he's left behind on the road. In seconds the truck is out of sight, the engine whining into the distance. The road grows quiet; there is no other traffic; the mist rolls in.

I angle the bike into the hedge, ease the pack off my shoulders and walk back up the road. The crates have fallen right before the bend, will be invisible to drivers from the town side until they are on top of them. Closer, I can see that they've both burst open; that their dark contents are spilling over the road. I can't make out what it is at first: coal, maybe, or turf, but as I near the spill, I see that the dark mass is moving of its own accord; the crates are heaving with something alive. The road is crawling with crabs. The brown creatures scuttle out sideways and spread across the highway, legs scissoring, blue pincers raised, their red eyes shuttling from side to side: velvet swimmers from the island, the most vicious kind there are. I shiver in the cool air. The crabs make for the hedges on both sides of the road. I watch as the first of them scurries into the grass and then I remember my camera. Evangeline will love this: escapee sea creatures, her kind of story. I am standing on the verge in the fog, wondering if they will make it back down the cliffs to the sea, photographing the strange retreat, when I feel my phone buzz in my pocket. I know who it is without looking at the screen.

'Ella?' my father says. 'Where are you?' I look through the trees towards the sea and down the hill to the town, but everything has been swallowed up by fog. I could be marooned on a cloud, or on an island the size of what I can see. I feel the panic begin to rise in me. 'Ella?' he says again. 'Ella? Are you okay? Just tell me where you are.' The air around shimmers, the earth makes a fractional shift. I have the sudden conviction that I have stood here before, looking down at the sloping road, at the smashed crates, the circling fog, the escaping crabs, impossible though that may be. Then I hear another voice behind my father's, Evangeline's, quiet, distracted by something, only half-engaged: cutting out or pasting in or colouring at the table.

'Ask my Ella if she got me a picture,' I hear her say. 'Tell her I'm waiting for her.'

The moment passes, the world realigns.

'Ella?' my father's voice again, walking away from my sister now, trying to disguise his concern. 'Ella, please, tell me what's happening.'

A sound escapes me, a laugh or a cry; I can't be certain which. 'You wouldn't believe it,' I hear myself say, surprised at the sound of my own voice. 'Tell Evangeline I've got her a picture. Tell her I'll see her soon.'

I slip the phone into my pocket; pack the camera back in my bag. I cross the road to where the crates lie and drag them into the verge. There isn't a single creature left. The mist is beginning to thin. Through the trees I can see the ferry back out of the harbour and turn around in the bay. I feel for the key in my pocket, the fob of smooth polished glass. It's too late now to go to the island. I'll go another day. I pick up the bike and climb back on and I cycle through the thinning mist in the direction from which I came.

# A Fuss


Rosa is at Connolly Station, in the waiting room for the Enterprise. The train is at the platform but is not yet boarding. She sits on a moulded plastic seat with her back to the glass partition that gives on to the railway lines, her rucksack tucked underneath, her head turned a little to the left towards the exit, her eyes on the railway staff who are milling around the train. Light slants in through the girdered station roof and casts arched shadows on to the tiled flooring beneath. She can still hear the drumming of the rain. There are only a few people in the waiting room, most of them in business suits, busy scrolling hand-held devices, answering messages, working on the move. There will be plenty of space on the train.

It is March, Friday, late afternoon. It means she will only miss a day and a half of work from the college library. Her manager was sympathetic, generous, when the phone call came through. It's three days' leave for a dead parent, more if she needs it but she won't need even that. She'll travel back on Monday, the day after the funeral. Her mother has learned not to depend on her; she has sisters of her own close by, one brother, a legion of nephews and nieces. By now the farmhouse kitchen will be steaming with pots of soup, water boiling in kettles for tea. They are all practiced in the theatre of mourning. Her part in it will be pivotal but small, a walk-on only. It will require a few rehearsed words, a modicum of self-control, limited exertion. She knows what is expected of her. She will be able to do it.

She has not changed out of her working clothes of neat black trousers, low-heeled shoes, a pale turtleneck sweater. It is not unsuitable attire for a wake. She has been told by her senior female colleagues that she dresses too old for her years, that she should wear make-up, style her hair; invest in a flash of colour. She overheard one of them once as she walked into the staffroom say something about a plain-clothes nun. She knows they were talking about her, but she does not wish to invite unwanted attention. Monochrome is fine. Celibacy, in her opinion, is vastly underrated.

Her uncle Colm will be waiting for her at the little red brick station wearing his dark wool coat that he keeps for such occasions. He had proposed to drive to Dublin to collect her but she had said there was no need. There would be things for him to do at home, arrangements to be made. She would get the train, catch the connection in Belfast, be in Knockarlet in the time it would have taken him to make the journey to her. He will shake her hand, offer to take her bag, say he is sorry for her trouble, which will be a strange thing to say, since it's his trouble too, but there will be no point in disputing with him the agreed hierarchy of loss. He will not kiss or embrace her. That's not the kind of family they are. He will say it's a terrible shock. You hear of these tragedies but you never expect them to visit your own door. Her father worked with beasts his whole life, he'll say, and never once made a mistake. He knew not to get between a heifer and her calf when the blood was up. They think that he must have tried to move away, caught his foot on something, an exposed root maybe, down there at the bottom of the low field, or went over on his ankle in the soft ground. They think he must have hit his head off the old enamel bath the cattle use as a drinking trough. He was not a young man, that is true, but still, and he won't finish the sentence because the sentence doesn't need finishing. She's already heard it all. No one wants to dwell on the circumstances, newsworthy though they are. No one wants to think of him lying face down, trampled into the rain-soaked earth by his own herd. It's not the kind of histrionic end they would have wanted for him in the family. They'd have preferred it if God had called him quietly, at home, in his own bed or in the armchair by the range with his feet up on the brown velvet stool. It would have been no less of a loss but they could have managed that more readily. They don't want to be an item in the local news. They're not the kind of family that likes a fuss.

Because it's her uncle's way, he will talk the whole road to the farm, but he will not say that Rosa, his sister's only child, born late to her and her husband and considered by them a blessing and a marvel always, that she should have come home to them more often, because that's not the kind of man he is; he's not the interfering kind. He will drive her up the ridged concrete road that rises from the bay, past sodden fields and dripping hedges and the bank of black-wrapped bales that will sit like mourning gifts at the side of the barn and he will say that he's never seen a March like it for rain, that there couldn't be a drop more water left in the sky. She'll wipe her feet on the thick coir mat at the kitchen door. She'll shake hands with the aunts and uncles and cousins. She'll find her mother by the open coffin in the front room with the lid propped like a great oaken kite against the pink flowered wallpaper, with her feet placed squarely on the dark red carpet, the worn part concealed, belatedly, by an unsuitable rug. Her mother will take Rosa's hands in hers and press them, and run her thumbs across the knuckles. She will not make a scene. They both know how to behave in order to get through this. They'll sit side-by-side on borrowed chairs and sip tea out of china cups that haven't seen daylight for years, not since her mother's mother was waked. They'll nibble at sandwiches that have arrived ready-made, packed into loaf bags, ferried in by neighbours; they'll nod and shake hands and thank people for coming and agree that it's a shock; they'll search long-unseen faces for some clue to recognition and sit silent and bleary-eyed by the coffin during the lulls.

And at some point, maybe tonight, certainly by the end of tomorrow, the headmaster will come to offer his condolences and she and her mother will shake his hand and say the same things to him. And when they have dispensed with the formalities, he will ask about her work in the library and she will say yes, she enjoys it, that the hours suit her, that she likes to be among books. And she knows her mother will be thinking about the day that she and Rosa sat together in that same room with the pink flowered wallpaper and the dark red carpet, when Rosa told her all the things he'd done to her in the classroom after school. When her mother had said that she must have been mistaken, that she must have dreamt it or have seen something filthy on TV, something she'd no business to see, for such a thing could not be countenanced between a child and the master who was tutoring her in his own time for the grammar school exam. And the whole time he is standing there, nodding, she will be remembering the smell of him, of cigarettes and chalk and bad teeth, and the roughness of his rag nail fingers, and his breath coming out, short, frantic, like a burrowing dog, and the way the light slanted in through the glazing bars of the high window and made a cage on the wooden schoolroom floor. And she will remember the important lesson she learned from this, from him and from her mother, that it is more agreeable to be quiet than to make a fuss by telling the truth. And on Sunday, when they've carried her father out and prayed over him, and put him back into the ground but civilly, this time, clad in oak and wearing his good suit and tie, then she will be able to go back to her quiet life in the busy city where it is possible to be alone with a bricked-up chimney of a heart without anyone remarking on it. She plans her route through the wake and funeral with military precision so that there will be no surprises, no unanticipated emotion to ambush her in the days ahead.

The automatic doors of the Enterprise waiting room glide soundlessly open and in shuffles a little white-haired lady in a purple felt beret, carrying awkwardly in both hands a red and yellow carpet bag, the base of which is almost dragging on the ground. She is wearing a white shaggy coat that reaches to her shins, what looks like a pair of soft black dancing pumps on her feet. She does not look to left or right. There are plenty of empty seats, but she walks straight past

Rosa and plumps down with an exaggerated sigh on to the plastic chair to her immediate left, drops the bag at her feet. Rosa looks past her towards the exit. The train is still not boarding.

'I'm raging,' says the little woman, uninvited, as if she and Rosa are mid-conversation, as if Rosa has asked her what is wrong. 'I shouldn't have brought the carpet bag for it's far too heavy to carry.'

A woman dressed in a pale grey jacket opposite raises her eyes from her screen, glances over at them. Rosa feels scrutinised. She turns her head slightly towards the little woman, manages what she hopes is an unencouraging smile.

'The wheelie case is far easier to manage,' she says in an accent that may once have been northern. 'Only I don't like to arrive with it, for it's far too big for a weekend visit and I don't want the nephew and his wife getting a fright and saying to themselves, "Has she no notion of going home?"' She digs a surprisingly sharp elbow into Rosa's side and throws her head back for a guffaw. The woman in the suit glances over again, raises her eyebrows, a smile playing about her lips. Rosa looks again towards the exit, willing for the signal to board. 'The condiments,' the little woman whispers suddenly to Rosa, bringing her face in close, enunciating each word, 'are electronic, button-operated, for one-touch grinding. Perfect for old arthritic hands. I couldn't resist them. Half price in Baxter's.'

Rosa risks a glance at her. Small brown eyes look out from under grey eyebrows. Her face is heavily made-up in what her mother used to call pan-stick, a half-hearted blotch of orange at her mouth, as though she has tentatively kissed a lipstick, a smear of green on her eyelids. The hat is secured above each ear by a silver hairclip, each ending in a diamante star. Her earrings are a pair of purple felt flowers pierced through with a silver stud, and now that she's closer, Rosa can see two darker purple flower-shaped patches where these must have been removed from the hat. The little woman leans down; snaps open the mouth of the bag between her feet. 'And now I know why they were cheap,' she says. 'The pepper mill is stuck—won't shift for love nor money. Six triple A batteries it takes and I've changed them twice. I'll soon have my whole pension spent. The nephew'll get it sorted, though, he's what you'd call a mechanical genius, has his head under the hood of a tractor every time you turn your back. I've told him all about it. He can't wait to get a look at them.' Cushioned among cardigans and bed socks, a toiletry bag, a pink shower cap, sit two pale wooden mills, each of them about a foot in length. 'I'm daft in the head,' she says to Rosa. 'I needn't have brought the salt mill, it's working fine. Only I don't like to separate the pair.'

She snaps the bag shut, straightens up, looks Rosa right in the eye. 'Thirteen years the husband's dead this October.' Though Rosa hasn't made to speak, she waves a hand to silence her. 'Everyone has their grief. Plus, it wasn't the first death I've had to endure, though it was mercifully sudden, a heart attack, and not like the children—I'll spare you the details.' You'd think she would be used to it by now, she says, but it's not the kind of thing you ever get used to, really. 'Still,' she says, tugging her hat down lower with both hands, checking the hairgrips are in place, 'better to have loved and lost, you know the rest yourself.' She'd had an awful time of it trying to locate her northern bus pass, she says, only where do you think she found it, in the sterling purse, of course! Some younger wiser version of her had left it there for her old senile brain to find. Not that she'll need it. The nephew will ferry her about. And now here's the train boarding at last. She reaches for the handles of the bag.

Rosa stands. 'Do you need a hand?' she says.

'No, no, dear. I can manage on my own,' and off she waddles, towards the train.

Rosa pulls her rucksack out from under her seat, walks slowly behind the little figure, keeping her distance, watches as she struggles up the step from the platform onto the train, sees that she has settled into a table seat, is shrugging her arms out of her coat. Rosa walks on to the next carriage, finds a quiet spot, sits down at the window, facing the direction of travel, puts her rucksack down on the seat beside her. She takes out a book, borrowed last minute from the library, glances at the blurb on the back cover. It's the story of a love affair, not her usual choice, but the writer is one she's read before. She had thought it would put the journey in. The train slips out of the station. She runs her hand over the glossy cover, tries to focus on the print.

When the train pulls up in Newry, Rosa still has not opened the book. Outside on the platform, in the grey light, stands a big man in green wellies, an unzipped anorak, cable-knit sweater, a peaked cap on his head. He is looking up and down the platform and then a broad smile breaks out on his face and he walks forward to meet the little white-haired lady with the heavy carpet bag. He wraps his two big arms around her and lifts her off the ground and she laughs and slaps him half-heartedly on the chest until he sets her down. He grabs the bag, crooks his elbow in a theatrical gesture and she slips her arm into his. The two of them exit the station, linked, talking and laughing, she with her little head raised up to look at him, he with his big head bent to look down at her.

Rosa closes her tired, stinging eyes. The engine idles in the station. She feels a little sickened by the smell of diesel and now there is a pain starting above her eye. She leans her head against the cool of the window, hears the soft sigh as the carriage doors close, feels the shudder through the glass as the train moves off again. Something drops on to the book in her lap. When she opens her eyes, she sees that it's a bead of water, that it has fallen on to the word 'hold', that it is distorting a little the print, enlarging the word like a lens. As she dabs it away with her finger, another drop falls, and another. She puts her hand to her face and finds that her cheeks are wet. She tries to dry them with her fingers but the tears roll down, unbidden. Half-blinded, she gropes in her rucksack for a tissue but now there is a sound like someone gasping for air, great rasping sobs coming out of her mouth and shaking her whole frame. She has not made provision for this. This is not part of the plan. She doesn't know if she's crying for the little woman with the carpet bag heavy with condiments, or for her father who went out in the morning, not knowing he wouldn't come back that day, or for her mother who will never get over this, no matter how attentive her relatives are, or for herself, for the lack of love in her life, because she hasn't allowed it in. She pats her face with the tissue. After a little while, the sobs subside. She looks out the window at the factory buildings and the flyovers and the desolate, puddled lanes, at barbed-wire fences and mossy banks, at a burst of yellow whin on a hillside in the distance. The leafless trees along the track are choked with ivy. They reach up their straggly finger-bone branches and proffer dark clumps of nest like shadows on an x-ray. The power lines are strung with roosting crows. The sky is a strange green hue. From behind a barn, something rises, like a handful of soil thrown high into the air, then just at the point at which it should fall, it takes shape into a flock of starlings, turns, rises higher, dissolves into the darkening sky. She is travelling between the lights, a thing her father told her was dangerous to do. And she still has miles to go.

# The House of the Quartered Door

Gina arrives at the airport on the western side of the island but her luggage does not arrive with her. She has not done the sensible thing and packed overnight necessities in her carry-on bag. She will have to make do for tonight. She is tired as she climbs the steps of the airport bus, and a little disorientated, like she's put something down and forgotten where she left it, like she's travelling unnaturally light.

It's six o'clock in Sardinia, five o'clock back home. The house there will be as she left it; the dishwasher will have finished its cycle; the tea towel will have dried on the handle of the cupboard door. In an hour or so, Rob will come in and strip out of his farm clothes and boots in the back porch. He won't shout hello; he knows she's not there. It was his idea for her to go: the heat, the light would help her, he said, she needed a rest after all she had been through. His mother's death had taken it out of them both, but Rob had the farm to see to. Gina should go, he had said, before the new teaching term started. So she went.

He'll shower and dress and come through to the kitchen and flick on the lights because even though it's August the weather has been so grey with them and he doesn't like the gloom. He'll find the leftover chilli in the fridge, carry it to the microwave, thumb the buttons to start. He'll click on the radio to hear the news; the switch for the kettle will be next. If she'd left him the note, that's where she would have left it, propped up against the kettle. Such an old-fashioned thing, a hand-written letter, but this is not a subject for text or email and a conversation is out of the question. She had promised Annie that she would never tell him, but lately she has been feeling a growing weight, the need to unburden herself. So she had written the letter and packed it into her suitcase. Later she will decide what to do. It's strange to think of him at home in an hour, at the time that it is where she is now. Sixty minutes; fifteen hundred miles; another world away.

The house in Sardinia stands on the south side of a small cobbled square. Its façade of pale blue is skirted with pink limestone. The houses on either side are painted lemon and green. She reaches the house via an entry that is too narrow for cars. As promised, the owners have left the key under a pot at the entrance. It was only for an hour or so, they said, and the neighbours would keep an eye on the place. There is one door in and out of the house. At first she thinks it is a half door, has a flash of memory of her grandfather's house in the glens, pale-legged hens picking through the yard, the old collie asleep, its face in a patch of sunlight by the barn. But when she turns the key in the lock she finds that the door opens in quarters. It's like unwrapping a present, or a puzzle, she thinks, like those folded snapdragons they used to make as children, the paper beaks opening in twos and fours to reveal each other's fortunes.

She steps into a cool, vaulted room, a tiled floor, a door that leads to a bathroom and a stone staircase that winds its way up the whitewashed wall to her right. Like all the other houses in the square it is a traditional tower dwelling, one room wide and three storeys high. On the first floor, the door opens off the top step and directly into a twin-bedded room. As she passes through, the door handle catches on her upper arm. The second floor houses a double bed; the kitchen is at the top of the house. There is no way of reaching the floor above or below without passing through each of the rooms. She chooses the second-floor bedroom to sleep in. There is bottled water in the fridge and she has oat bars in her bag. It's all she needs for now. She sends Rob a message to say she has arrived, opens the window and the shutters on to the square and lies down and closes her eyes. For weeks they have been slaves to hospital appointments, consultations, the grinding bedside wait. 'Ring me if you want to,' Rob has said, 'but take the time; sketch a bit. You don't do enough of that now.'

She wakes to the rumble of wheels over cobblestones. She has slept right through the night. She rises and leans out the window of the bedroom and spots a man in shirt sleeves crossing the square, dragging a suitcase, peering at house numbers, heading towards hers. This must be the taxi driver the airline has promised, restoring her to her things. She slips into her sandals, walks down the stairs to the quartered door, reaches it as he does, opens it to blinding light. She signs for the luggage and thanks him, pulls the bag inside. As she recloses the panels, she spots a yellow-haired woman on the roof terrace of the house in the opposite corner of the square, a cigarette in her hand, a phone to her ear, staring across with what seems like a glowering look. Gina locks the door and drags the case up the steps; is caught once again by the handle of the door on the first floor. In the room above, she unpacks what she needs, checks that the letter's still there.

From the window she watches the dark-skirted ladies of the square leave their doors carrying shopping bags and she goes out and follows them. In a neighbouring street she finds a bakery, a supermarket and buys what she needs. There is a café on the *corso*. The *barista* glances at her as she walks in. '*Mi dica!*' he says. She asks for a coffee, points at a brioche under the glass, sits down outside in the shade. The brioches sometimes have apricot jam at their centre, sometimes *crema*, sometimes no filling at all. She doesn't have the language to differentiate, and anyway, all of these are fine with her. It's a low risk sugar lottery. She doesn't mind what comes.

At noon she is sitting outside the door of the house, scratching with pencil and ink into the thick white paper of her sketch book, capturing the yellow building to the east of the square. A rose climbs in a thick, plaited vine out of a blue pot at the door, stretches its branches along electric cables, drops pink petals into the square. A pigeon picks through the cobblestones. The shafts of a wooden cart, abandoned in one corner, are draped with drying cloths. The door handle from the bedroom above has left a purple bruise on her upper arm the shape of a comma, or an apostrophe: a pause, or a sign of something missing, or of something belonging, perhaps. She keeps forgetting that the door handle is there, keeps catching herself on the same spot. She flicks back through the sketch book to the drawings from the weeks before, studies in pencil from the quiet hours she'd sat by Annie's bedside, scenes from the hospice window of tended lawns, rose gardens, planted beds, and one drawing that is at odds with the others, that looks inwards, into the room. She sees again the metal guards of the hospital bed, the IV tube, the wasted hand, the veins ruined with punctures, the darkened fingernails.

In the square, a stooped elderly man wearing glasses emerges from the house beside Gina's, nods a greeting, and sits down on a plastic chair with a book in his lap. This house, Gina has noticed, is wider than her rented house, a knock-through between two former dwellings, perhaps. A small fair-headed girl follows him out. He is teaching the child to count: words in a steady, rhythmic chant that the little girl repeats after him. Day-trippers wander through. They photograph the covered well at the northern end of the square, the pastel façades of the houses, the climbing rose. Footsteps echo over cobbles, voices reverberate around the walls. From the open windows of the kitchens comes the smell of freshly cooking *ragù*.

Two boys appear from the alleyway on the southern side of the square, aged about eight or nine, the taller, darker-skinned of the two with a flask on a strap slung over his shoulder, the smaller with some sheets of coloured paper gripped in his fist. The smaller boy lifts a hand in greeting towards the older man and the child, stops beside them, shouts '*Mamma!*' up to the second floor where a woman appears on the balcony above Gina. Gina does not understand all of the exchange that follows as the smaller boy holds up what she can see are printed fliers, but it is clear that he is asking for something that the mother will not grant. She is calm and measured in her returns to him as she questions the other boy. He mentions '*il mare*', '*la festa*': Gina understands that it's a visit to the fair at the beach that is being proposed, but the mother, though cordial, holds firm, seems to broker an agreement of some kind, and the older of the boys takes his leave.

The smaller boy goes into the house, chin lowered, the older man and the child following. Doors close, footsteps ring out on the stairs and a moment or two after, something flies over Gina's head into the square. She ducks instinctively, but when she looks up she sees that it is only a paper aeroplane, that it has glided as far as the cover of the well and has landed among the terracotta pots from which an array of succulents grow. The plane is followed by a second one, constructed, Gina can see now from another of the posters, and now there are the boy and the little girl on the balcony above, laughing, flying their coloured planes together. Gina has another flash of memory: her father the summer her mother had left, teaching her how to make paper planes: to fold a sheet of paper lengthways, turn two of the corners into the centre, and do the same again. Those planes they flew from the loft of the red barn out over the yard of her grandfather's house in the July evenings, until twilight brought the bats swooping out, the white darts competing with the dark. In the square in Sardinia, the boy seems to be bearing his disappointment equably, as though it is not unexpected, as though it will not deter him from trying again, perhaps tomorrow, since things, after all, can change.

The line of shade creeps closer to the house and begins to climb the walls. Gina watches with envy as the shadow grows out from the northern side of the square. By three the sun has reached the quartered door and it is too hot for her to sit outside. By five the kitchen window at the top of the house is bathed in heat. There are no balconies on this house. The kitchen window opens to a breast-high metal guardrail with curlicues in fleur-de-lis. When she leans on it to look into the square the hot metal burns into her bare arm. She closes the shutters. In the dim light she puts together a salad, eats curled up on the divan, with a glass of water at her side. That night she sleeps an untroubled sleep.

In the evening of the third day, the square in Sardinia is full of voices: a young woman spooning food to a baby in a high chair; residents exchanging pleasantries by open doors, enjoying the cooling air. From the kitchen Gina watches as the yellow-haired woman appears on the roof terrace opposite, moves like a sleepwalker towards the metal railing, leans over, calls down to the woman with the child. The child's mother raises her face and answers her, but places what looks like a protective hand behind the baby's head. Beyond the square are the sounds of engines; raised voices, barking dogs, warring cats. The people from the house beside Gina, the house of the paper aeroplanes, have placed a wooden trestle table and plastic chairs outside. The dark-haired boy is busy setting cutlery, the small girl helping him, the grandfather carrying plates and glasses. Then a small group arrives in the square, and Gina recognises the boy from the previous day, this time with a man and a woman and two smaller children alongside. The families greet each other and sit down together to eat.

When it is quite dark, the older, dark-clad women from the houses opposite emerge from the yellow rectangles of their doors and drag chairs out into the cool of the square. They call to each other from doorways, one approaches the covered well with a watering can and sprinkles a little water on the plants, another, much older woman, leans over the shafts of the cart, moving her lips in silent prayer, a string of beads threaded through her hands.

Gina is lying on the bed, reading, with the windows open and the lace panel moving in the breeze. Her eyes droop to the sound of the voices, the laughter outside, cutlery on dishes, clinking glasses. Then there is a shout, a woman's voice, angry, and the voices in the square below her quieten. When Gina goes to the window the yellow-haired woman is there on the roof terrace opposite, leaning over, shouting down. It is after midnight. The members of the little party below her are the only people left in the square. '*Certi individui,*' Gina hears her shout as she marches up and down the terrace: 'Certain people'; she is complaining about the noise, and something else about the children, the irritation of them. Silenced, the family and their guests stand, one by one, chairs scraping back across the cobbles, and carry dishes into the house. No one looks at the terrace opposite; no one answers her. Moments later, with kisses and lowered voices, the visiting family departs.

The bruise on Gina's arm gets bigger every day. She measures the passing of time by its rainbow of colours, through purple, then yellow, then green. On the fourth day, she is in the kitchen, washing up the breakfast dishes when she hears a yell outside in the square. From the window she can see the yellow-haired woman, leaning out of a window opposite, this time shouting at a thin-framed, curly-haired man below who is walking away from the house. He stops now, his head raised, looking up at the woman. She shouts again, the inflection rising, a question perhaps, the word '*mercato*' to which the man answers quietly, '*Sì*'. She shouts something else, dips in through the window, he turns away to walk on, then her head reappears and she seems to be asking him to wait, she seems to be considering something. She shouts again and he says 'OK', and she shouts another time, only now her voice is angrier and he says, '*Sì, sì, ho capito,*' and defeated, his head lowered, he returns to the house where the shouting grows louder and Gina can no longer hear his voice at all. It seems to Gina that whatever it is he is perceived to have done or has neglected to do, he's being punished for it now. The woman's voice rings around the walls of the square, shouting the same thing over and over. '*Capisci?*' Gina makes out and then, '*Zito!*' The rest Gina does not catch but the words keep coming and coming and she knows they must fall on him like a torrent, like a landslide, like a darkness. There is something not right, Gina thinks, with the woman. What hold does she have over him, over the people of the square? She thinks about her mother the night she left and all the other nights before, about the things she shouted at her father, about his voice, low, saying, 'Think of the child. Stay for her sake.' She had watched him carry the hurt of her mother's leaving around for years, like a basin too full of water, never allowing it to spill over, never wanting it to touch her. She had wondered, from time to time, that he had never looked for her, wondered what their life would have been if her mother had stayed.

Annie had been more mother to Gina than her own mother had ever been. In the twenty-five years that she had known her, they had grieved together over every one of Gina's lost pregnancies, over every deadly cramp that had bent her double, over the first spot of each monthly blood. Annie knew every anniversary of every baby that hadn't survived, shared the empty ache of her arms. When the news came through of Gina's father's death, it was Annie who had knelt beside Gina on the tiled kitchen floor, had cradled her while she sobbed, until Rob had made his way home. In the hospice, when Annie had stopped talking, Gina watched her eyes. She knew when she was too tired for visitors, when she wanted to have her hand held, when she needed to be turned in bed. She knew when Annie was desperate for a drink of water, though in the last days Gina hadn't been permitted to give her one. 'She's lost her swallow,' the thin-faced nurse had explained, 'there's a danger of aspiration.'

'So we watch her starve?' Gina had said and the nurse did not answer her. She was used, Gina guessed, to brittle relatives whose nerves were frayed at the ends. Gina moistened Annie's lips with glycerine, propped a rolled pillow under her ankles to raise the tender flesh at her heels, to ease the sores where fragile bones had threatened to break through paper-thin skin. They had talked about this point, the two of them, Annie had made Gina listen, had extracted a promise from her.

'I want to have some say in it,' Annie had said. Gina

knew what she was telling her that last day when she locked eyes with her: that Annie had had enough; that it was time.

'Are you sure?' Gina had asked her. 'Are you ready?' and Annie had nodded and taken Gina's hand and with her ruined heel pushed the rolled pillow out from under her foot, and all the love she had for Gina and for Rob and for her unborn grandchildren had glistened in her eyes.

'She went quickly in the end,' the thin-faced nurse had said. 'It's a blessing when it happens that way.' The nurse's pockets were ironed flat like there was nothing to hide and she didn't look Gina in the eye.

On the last night on the island, Gina dreams that there is a knock at the quartered door and when she goes barefoot down the stone stairs to open it, Annie is there, unbidden, smiling, looking a little lost. 'Annie,' Gina says to her, 'You're here.' And Annie smiles and says 'Yes,' like she doesn't know where she is at all but is happy, notwithstanding. Her face is shining and her white hair is arranged in a way that Gina has never seen it, caught up in two untidy plaits and sticking out either side of her head. Gina reaches to take her hands in hers but Annie is carrying something, what looks like a little plastic takeaway dish. She hands it to Gina and when Gina prises open the lid, there is a tiny baby curled inside, bald and blind, pink and perfect, not cold and not crying at all.

Gina wakes and goes to her case and takes out the note that she did not leave by the kettle for Rob. It was the selfish act of a guilty conscience to write it, she thinks. There is no need for Rob to know what she did, what Annie had asked her to do. She folds the sheet of paper lengthways once, opens it, folds two corners in, does the same again. She keeps on folding the way her father had taught her, scoring the paper flat with her thumbnail. Her fingers remember what to do. The nose of the plane is knife sharp, the inked words now blurred, illegible. She climbs the last flight of steps to the kitchen, opens the shutter, leans out over the cool of the metal guardrail, raises the paper plane above her head and throws with all her strength. She watches as it soars out over the cobbled square, beyond the covered well, out into the darkness of the night.

Gina has to leave to catch the bus for her flight. It is early, just after five, and the heat is already beginning to rise. She dresses in a sleeveless top, ties a sweater around her waist. Her case is too heavy to lift and carry. She has no option but to roll it over the cobbles and it is exactly as loud in the still morning air as she expects it to be. She is halfway across the square when the window opens in the house opposite and the yellow-haired woman leans out and shouts. Gina stops at the voice but then starts walking again. What else is she to do? And then there's the bang of a door and the woman is there, the first time all week that Gina has seen her down here in the square, slippered and in a pale night dress, her hair flying, cheeks livid, shouting into Gina's face, pointing at the suitcase, at the sky, at her watchless wrist, enraged at the noise, at the early hour, at Gina's inability to appreciate the full brunt of her tirade. Gina looks into the woman's eyes and they are blood-shot, ruined. There is no reason there. She wonders if the woman will strike her and if she does what she will do. The windows of all the other houses remain shuttered. Gina picks up her case by the handle to demonstrate its weight, sets it down again. She does not shrug her shoulders since that might indicate a lack of concern. Now that she's close to the woman, she seems less frightening, full of bluster in fact. There is a sadness there, a desperation, but Gina has to go. She holds out her hand to the woman and says the only word she can think of. '*Arrivederci*,' Gina says and the woman stares at her, hard, and does not take her hand.

Then Gina sees that she is looking at her shoulder, at the mark that the door handle has left there, and the woman draws in her breath. She reaches out and touches Gina's arm, traces the shape of the bruise with her fingertips and her eyes fill with pain. From behind her, in the doorway of the house, there is a movement and the man appears, the one that the woman had so berated in the days before. He comes up to them and takes the woman, gently, by the elbow and says, '*Vieni Lucia, vieni con me*,' and the woman turns to him and says something and points to Gina's arm. '*Sì*,' he says, '*si è fatta male*.' *She's hurt herself. Come now, with me.* For a moment the woman's eyes stay on Gina's before she allows herself to be turned and then her gaze drops and she walks back to the house with him. Gina grips the handle of the suitcase and starts walking again, dragging the case behind her. As she reaches the entry she glances back, sees the couple caught in the doorway, alone, in the sulphurous lamplight of the empty, cobbled square.

There are a myriad of ways, she thinks, in which we contrive to hurt the people we love and to hurt ourselves.

And then Gina goes home.

# The Cure for Too Much Feeling

With Rita it had begun gently, a slight quiver in the hand, acid in her stomach, a tight sense of weariness in the afternoons when she had finished an early shift at work. She made an appointment to see the doctor and described the symptoms to him. He tested her heart, her blood pressure, cholesterol levels, good and bad, made enquiries as to the efficiency of her digestive system, suggested that, maybe, she should consider taking a break. He mentioned a food diary. 'You may have developed an allergy,' he said. 'It sometimes happens in later life.' So she took time off her job at the mini-mart and booked a coach trip to Connemara where it rained non-stop for three days and her symptoms grew worse. The people on the bus were full of grief. Every time one of them sat down beside her to tell of the loss of a spouse or a dog or of a winning Lottery ticket, she experienced a twinge of pain in her chest, a sensation like a growing knot at the back of her throat. At the Twelve Pins, where a widow confessed that she had never liked her husband of more than forty years, Rita felt the sweat gather between her shoulder blades, the skin on her upper arms begin to rise and tingle, and had to ask to be let out of the coach for a breath of air. Bit by bit, she began to believe that her growing trouble was not related to the consumption of dairy or gluten or (God forbid) potatoes, but was a newly developed susceptibility to other people's misery. She had never experienced any bother like this before. She suspected there was no antidote. She ate a cooked breakfast in the hotel every morning and returned to Belfast several pounds heavier. From then on, she resolved to avoid people and their stories of woe as much as she was able.

There was no husband to trouble the surface of Rita's life. She'd had a child once, a girl, but she'd given her up almost immediately. She was very small and wrinkled with startling black hair that stuck out from the side of her head like a crow's wing, and she cried, Rita remembered, for no reason at all. The child was the consequence of a rainy evening in the back of a white Mark 111 Ford Cortina in 1976 when her after-school shift at the chippy had ended and the owner (Mr Percy, red-bearded, married with three young boys) had eyed the laddered knee of her black uniform tights and said it was a shocking bad night to be walking home. He had a four-door saloon with synchromesh gearbox and double wishbone suspension, four more inches of extra interior width on the earlier model, the Mark 11. She remembered very clearly the walnut-trimmed dashboard, the bucket seats, his freckled fingers on her leg, working the threads of her laddered tights apart into a hole big enough to slide his hand and then his arm through, round the back of her thigh, up inside her underwear. She didn't remember agreeing to anything, but she hadn't wanted to appear ungrateful. It was raining very hard by then. She got beard rash all the way down her neck and had had to stuff her ruined tights and knickers in the Doric, for fear her mother would see them, but her mother figured it out herself when the waistband on Rita's school skirt had had to be let out a second time.

She was sent away to an aunt in Belfast where such matters were more easily explained. After they took the baby away, she got a job in the ciggie factory where her aunt worked, with a good bonus and free packs of fags and what if she did stink of tobacco most of the time? The money smelled only of money. She stayed away from men because the episode in the Cortina had been surprising, messy and, to be honest, a little painful, and she didn't want any more babies to trouble her. Her aunt had been glad of the company; her uncle was away at sea. They had to move house when work started on the motorway; the whole street was being demolished, but she doesn't know if her aunt ever gave her uncle their new address because Rita never laid eyes on him and then the aunt smoked herself into an early grave and there was Rita with a job and a house and what more could you want? She got a good payout when the factory closed, took a few shifts in the mini-mart to get her out of the house.

She couldn't work out what had caused the change. Up until the age of fifty-six she'd been as immune to other people's troubles as was everyone else around her. It was a kind of creeping sickness. She was too embarrassed to go back to the doctor and tell him what she now knew, so she adopted strategies for survival. In the days and weeks after the Connemara trip, Rita learned how to carry herself careful. Open fires were to be avoided, she found; they drew stories out of people, and pubs were bad too, of course, for alcohol is a known tongue-loosener, and as for a pub with an open fire, forget about it, her stomach would never stick it. Rita had an open fire in her little yellow-bricked terraced house, but she put a pillow up the chimney and had an electric bar fitted. It was much cleaner without the soot. She didn't have to miss out on a drink: the mini-mart had started doing gin and tonic, ready-mixed in those handy cans that you could keep in the fridge and pop open when the mood took you and the tonic never went flat and the can was always cold.

Still, it was a loss to find that she was no longer able to nibble at tragedy the way that she had done before, couldn't say, 'Isn't it shocking about that poor woman the other morning, black ice on the road early?' and then set it aside and get on. She couldn't hear, 'They're sitting up with Dan Reilly,' and nod and go about her business. She was laid low by other people's misery, it sapped her energy, brought her out in a rash. She couldn't sit down to enjoy the news. Even a second onscreen of Syria or Gaza or a Greek island beach would have her clutching at her stomach with cramps. She was near-crippled by the look in the children's dark eyes, the sorrow of it seeping into her. She began to avoid local radio in the mornings when it was all phone-ins and shouting to outdo each other's hurt, and if she listened sometimes in the afternoons to the anniversary and birthday requests, she was always careful to switch off at five minutes to the hour, before the bulletins came on. She tuned in to Classical FM, though she had to be careful around a violin solo. Once she found herself a few bars in to Beethoven's 'Funeral March' before she realised what it was. She just made it to the dial in time. A-flat was not a good chord for her. She didn't read newspapers or true-life magazines. She was untroubled by the vagaries of the internet. She would occasionally flick through the mail-order catalogues and imagine the lives of the cardigan-ed, white-toothed people there. She averted her eyes from the head-scarfed woman who sold the homeless magazine outside the bank in town. She stopped her ears at bus stops, scissored through every charity appeal that dropped through her door, but despite her careful efforts, every once in a while something would seep through. A chance remark overheard, a hand on her arm at the till in the mini-mart, a glance in the window of the TV shop where the largest screens were tuned to twenty-four-hour news, and then it could take several episodes of stock-piled Val Doonican shows to restore her to herself. She had been managing fairly well until the day there came a knock on the door and Rita's chest began to tighten even before she opened it.

It was the girl, of course, although she was no longer a girl: forty years old she would have been by then. Rita had always known it was a possibility that she might turn up. That same lick of black hair; something in her thin lips of the set of her own mother's mouth; she knew her straight away. She asked her in and gave her tea and told her she didn't know who the father was, which was only half a lie, since she had never heard Mr Percy's first name. It showed her in a bad light, she knew, but it seemed kinder that way. Supposing that he was still alive, supposing that the girl managed to locate him, Rita didn't reckon that Mr or Mrs Percy or their—by now middle-aged—sons would want anything to do with either one of them. So the girl—the woman—whose name was Anna (a neat name, easily remembered, only two letters, back-to-back) went away again.

On Sundays Rita took a bus to the south side of the

city, where she was unlikely to meet anyone she knew or anyone who knew her, and where she could walk in peace in the green areas without anyone passing remarks. She was coming through Botanic Gardens one day in January, the cold biting at her cheeks, when a sudden shower of sleety rain drove her up the incline to shelter under the grey bulk of the museum. She'd never been inside, but it was draughty under the concrete canopy that hung like a lip over the entrance, and the rain bouncing off the steps and down through the dripping trees and off the head of the statue of Kelvin by the park gates was lowering her mood. And, she remembered, it was free to go in.

She found herself in a large open space, the ceiling more than fifty feet up, concrete and glass and steel on all sides. She decided to take a ride in the lift, to act like someone who'd intended to make the visit. On the fourth floor, she stood for a while at the glass balustrade, looking down through the dizzying atrium to the ground floor below, at the purple shirts of the museum staff, at a woman seated in a lime green anorak, leaflets fanned like palm fronds on the glass-topped table beside her. She watched as people crossed the foyer, shaking umbrellas, checking signs for floor descriptions, finding their way. The walls and ceiling were a blinding white. Moments later, the lift pinged to a halt to her left, and a group emerged: three women, half a dozen small children. One of them, a boy of two or three, fell back, dragging his mother by the hand, shouting to her that he wanted to go back in the lift, but she walked on and as he dropped to the floor, his cries began to echo and bounce off the walls until the space was filled with a hundred children crying. Rita gripped the balustrade, its bevelled edge marked with dozens of small fingerprints, and forced herself to stand there, with the light bouncing off the glass, and the cries ringing round her. Then the mother picked the child up and balanced him on her hip and carried him through the heavy wooden door to the adjoining gallery that closed solidly behind them.

A sign beyond the lift indicated an exhibition of portraits in the direction opposite to the one in which the crying child had been taken. Rita liked to look at pictures of people; there weren't many places where you could study faces safely. Even in a café or at the bus stop, people sometimes caught you staring, took it as an invitation to speak.

She made her way to the gallery, but the portraits were not at all what she had been expecting. They were modern for a start. She had imagined pearls and ruffs and silks but these were all hoodies and scowls and tattoos and, God preserve us, an entirely naked woman, straight browed, navel-pierced, gazing out, the delta of her shorn pubic hair precisely at Rita's eye-level. What were they thinking, hanging that up on a Sunday for anyone to see? Rita coloured and turned her eyes away, walked quickly past, putting safe distance between her and the unabashed woman, stopped to slow her heart in front of a painting of a man in a red v-neck sweater in a blue wallpapered room.

They were so lifelike, some of them; you couldn't tell they were paintings at all, even up close they looked like enlarged photographs, there was hardly any sign of marks, but 'oil on canvas' it read on the wall panel, or 'oil on linen' or 'on gesso' or 'on board', so they were paintings, all of them, she checked every one as she passed. She felt a little hoodwinked by this. She thought it was a bit of a cheat. Where were the brush strokes, the thickened slabs of paint, the pencilled marks, the rubbings out? She wanted, she realised, honest artifice, evidence of work. It was only in the blades of grass in the background, or in the leaves or the petals or occasionally, in the eyes, in the way the white oil of reflected light hit the liquid black of the iris that you could tell that this was a worked thing. 'Because the eye is a giveaway,' she said to herself, and then realised she'd spoken aloud. When she looked around, the museum attendant showed no sign of having heard her.

She had completed a circuit of the room and was nearing the exit when she noticed a painting she had missed on her way in, in her hurry past the naked gazing woman. This one, entitled *Washing Mother's Hair*, presented two figures, both side-on, inclined towards each other, their faces in profile, oblivious to the onlooker. The scene was viewed as if through the frame of an open bathroom door, an elderly woman seated on the edge of the bath, her head bowed over the sink; another woman, younger but not young, facing her, pouring water from a white plastic mixing jug over the other woman's head. The hair was plastered to the old lady's scalp, the bones of her neck and of her small skull showing through under pink skin. A yellow towel lay over her shoulders, over the white of the full slip she was wearing, the skin on her upper arms crinkled as tissue paper, the veins on her legs and on her slippered feet, raised and wormed and blue. With one hand, she had gathered the corners of the towel under her chin like a shawl; the other hand gripped the wash hand basin, like she feared she was in danger of falling. Her daughter's dark hair was tied in a low knot at the nape of her neck from where it sprang, curly, down her back. The girl looked weary, her back bent in an uncomfortable position, stretching to reach over her mother's bowed head to rinse the water from her hair. There was something about the composition that held Rita, something ritual in the scene, in the triangulation of the two figures over the bathroom sink, their physical closeness in the cramped room, the daughter's right hand, pouring water, her left hand outstretched, like a benediction, something easy between the two of them that said, 'We know who we are to one another and this is what we do.' It seemed to Rita that if she could stand there for long enough, if they would let her stay, if the purple-shirted attendant would put out the lights and lock up the gallery and go home and leave her there, that she might witness a quiet miracle. The girl might squeeze the last drop of water out of her mother's damp hair and set the jug down on the deep-tiled window sill, beside the toothbrush and the shampoo bottle and the aloe vera plant that was growing there out of a used margarine tub; she might lift the yellow towel and twist it round her mother's head, and slide an arm under the old woman's elbow to ease her up and steady her, might turn her round to face the bathroom door, and walk her straight out of the picture frame, past Rita, and up a darkened hallway to a cushioned chair by a crackling fire where the old woman's hair would dry and settle into soft white curls. And it seemed to Rita that she would then be privy to the sort of act of casual intimacy that passes unannounced in homes everywhere where people are tired or hurting or weak and still going about the everyday business of caring for one another and of being loved. But Rita didn't stay. She turned on her heel away from the painting and walked out the gallery door, down the four flights of stairs to the ground floor, past the milling people with their spattered raincoats and their dripping umbrellas, and out of the museum into her careful life and the still falling rain.

# Nomad

Before you ask, I don't know where she is. The last I saw of her was at your brother's place in Limone, the time he lent me the house. She must have phoned Neil; she knew I would be there. Have you spoken to him?

I got back to Neil's place one night, a bit worse for wear, I must admit, and there she was, asleep on the couch. I'd spent the evening with the old boys in the square, shuffling dominoes around a bottle of grappa, timing the moves between shots, calling it research for the book. That's the thing about a game like dominoes—you don't need any language to play. You can interpret the gestures quite clearly, and as for the under-the-breath swearing, it's probably best not to know. You'd be surprised how contentious things can get over a mound of little black tiles. 'The bone yard', they call it, when they have them all laid out, facedown. 'The bone yard', think of that. I was watching my fellow players: the gnomish, white-haired one with the silver heart on a shoelace round his neck; the one they call Gilberto who never takes off his moped helmet, who checks between every move that the strap is secure under his chin; the one with the moustache that curls over his lip, open pores on his nose. I was looking for stories, failing to find them. It wasn't the language that was the barrier; there was something else standing in the way. I got the uncomfortable feeling, now and again, looking at them, that I was looking at my disappointed self.

I stumbled home in the early hours; found that I hadn't locked the patio doors. Don't tell Neil. That's what sun and alcohol do to you—they make you lazy, careless about the detail. It's not a good mix for a writer. It's lucky I have nothing to steal. I don't know why I went there. Some romantic notion, I suppose, about cloudless skies clearing the head, when we all know that grey light and shadow are so much more conducive to making things up. I slouched into the salon and there she was, curled up on the divan the way she's always slept, like a comma, knees up to her chin. Fia, the wanderer: always unexpected; always a welcome sight. She must have heard me come in; you know how watchful she is, but she didn't speak. I covered her up with a throw, locked the doors, crawled into bed.

I got up around eight, my head pounding, still breathing out the effects of the alcohol. I went into her and she lifted her head off the cushion, hair in her eyes and smiled up at me, superior. 'Morning, Greg,' she said, 'Good night?' Like it hadn't been months since we'd last met. No preamble, no account of herself. If anything, she looked like she was expecting some form of explanation from me.

She was thinner than the last time I'd seen her, that night of your birthday, and paler, dark shadows under her eyes. No make-up, feet bare, a pair of pumps kicked over the mat, one small black rucksack on the floor, and that tatty little bracelet you made for her from the braided wool of her red blanket, still on her arm after all this time. She kicked off the throw. She was wearing one of those sheath dresses, black, her pelvic bones showing through. It could have been off the peg, I don't know, white trim at the neck. You know that way she has of making everything look designer, no matter what the price. She got up and padded through to the bathroom. She has some kind of inbuilt homing device, I think, except it doesn't take her home, wherever that is now; it takes her to people she knows she can trust. Stepping stones, people like me, and you, and Neil. I don't know how many of us there are on the list, how much ground we cover.

I brewed some coffee, whisked up a batch of pancake batter, couldn't resist the theatre of plucking a lemon from the tree in the courtyard, though I knew she'd rib me for it. I stacked the pancakes the way she's always liked them, soaked in lemon juice, crunchy with sugar. She came back out of the bathroom wearing the black dress, her hair on her shoulders, wet. 'You're quite the continental,' she said, with that wry smile of hers, but she ate like she hadn't seen food in days.

Some guy she knew had sent for her in Milan, she said, wanted her on his arm for a big industry do. She'd gone, because she was between jobs and Milan was as good a place to find one as any. But there was no work ('The *gaunt* thing is over,' she said), and she tired of the man in the Valentino tux, discovered too late that the air ticket was one-way. She was watching me as she told me this, trying to get a rise out of me. I said nothing. I'm wise to her ways. She doesn't care about the situations she gets herself into. She's all for the movement, the lights, the adventure. She knows that when the shine wears off, she can always depend on her list.

She mentioned something about a music video, a magazine shoot, maybe. She didn't say where or when. She said something about heading south, following the arc of the sun. She dabbed her fingers in the grains of sugar from the counter top, picked up the squeezed lemon, examined the empty chambers like they held some kind of secret. I saw her slip a pip into the pocket of her bag. She hasn't broken that habit of collecting things. Remember the coloured paper clips, the endless chains she used to make, the obsession over the pattern repeat, the delays while she waited for a crucial yellow or blue? Maybe she's still doing that. Maybe we're her pattern repeat now: the places she feels safe; the people who love her, who look out for her, who'll be there for her no matter what. I offered her money and she took it. She scooped up her bag, said the world was very grey these days; she needed some sun on her skin. And then she left.

I went into the bathroom after she'd gone. The kidney-shaped prints of her wet feet were fading on the grey ceramic tiles. She'd left the damp towel bundled in the shower, the way people do in hotels where it's someone else's job to pick it up and launder it. In the steamed-up bathroom mirror, she'd traced a little tree, and a stick man in a cap, holding the hand of a little stick girl. And it made me think of those walks in the park, by the museum, do you remember, not long after she came to us? When we were still trying to figure out how much she'd witnessed at home; what she'd seen. Not that she ever held *my* hand; not that she ever allowed herself to touch *me*; but still, it made me think of that time, when she was small, when we were still married, when it felt like things could still turn out okay. And it felt like a sort of acknowledgement, that little drawing in the condensation, or a thank you, maybe, or the closest she would ever get to one.

That was three, maybe four months ago. I haven't heard from her since. I didn't stay long at Limone. The writing wouldn't come. I thought that stillness was what I needed to think, but it wasn't that at all. Maybe she and I have more in common than I thought; maybe we both need to move to survive. Try not to worry about her. There's no point in worrying. She's a survivor. If she's missing it's because she wants to be. She'll come back in her own time, when the sun moves north again. We'll see her when she needs something from us. She'll be with one of her list.

# Star Gazers

The long cupboard at the end of the kitchen bench is where the porridge oats are kept along with the porridge bowls and spoons. When I first came, I thought this was odd: in our flat the cereal is in one cupboard and the crockery is in another and the cutlery lives all together in a drawer.

'How many steps do you think that is, to make breakfast?' Mumma said.

'I don't know,' I told her. 'I never counted. Twenty, maybe, twenty-five?'

'Granda can only take a small number of steps. Even before the stroke he got into the habit of keeping things together that are used together. There's less searching for things,' Mumma said.

'What about lunch?' I asked her.

Mumma showed me the lunch cupboard: the bread and the tins of vegetable broth that Granda likes, the soup spoons and bowls and small plates.

'But what about guests and visitors?' I said. 'How do they know where to find things?'

'I don't think we need to worry about that, Cassie,' she said.

Ben could be classified as a visitor, or a guest, but Mumma says if anyone asks, Ben is an essential caregiver. Ben is the only person who is allowed in. He's been keeping an eye on Granda. It was him who phoned the ambulance the time Granda fell. They used to play cards together and now Ben comes on a Saturday night and plays cards with Mumma instead. He's tall and has dark curly hair and wears walking boots and a beanie hat. Mumma pulls out the green baize-topped table in the living room, the one with the folding scissor legs, and they play Gin Rummy and Jack Changes but not Poker and never for money, and always at a two-metre distance. Mumma could never defy Granda by playing Poker in the house, she says, even though Granda's asleep in the lower room and it would take a hurricane to wake him. Ben drinks one glass of spring water from the special pump tap that Granda had fitted at the kitchen sink. Ben's glass lives in the cupboard where the spare kitchen things are kept, but Ben never goes in the kitchen. What would Ben want in the kitchen? We have to be very careful, because of Granda.

Mumma and me like to dance in the kitchen when we're cooking the dinner. We turn the volume on the CD player up high. Mumma says Granda'd hear nothing over the TV anyway—he has it up full belt, muttering at the six o'clock news, at the R number going up and down, at the graphs, the statistics. We don't count the dancing steps; Mumma says dancing has nothing to do with conserving energy, dancing's all about expression. We like Aretha and Ella but 'Midnight Train to Georgia' is my favourite: Mumma does Gladys and I do the Pips, all three of them. I've learned the moves from YouTube but they're tricky, especially the walking backwards bit. Mumma says they used to call that 'moon walking' but it looks nothing like what the Apollo 11 astronauts did. That was a kind of running hop. I've watched all the footage, even the conspiracy theory stuff. The best part of 'Midnight Train' is the whistle: 'Whoo hoo!' Shortlegs doesn't join in. She lies under the long cupboard with her chin on her paws and watches us. I think she's worried we'll tread on her. Mumma says there are only four things in life that are of interest to Shortlegs and they are: running, sleeping, eating, and humping her bed. Dancing and space travel are not on the list. 'Do you not think she loves us?' I asked Mumma and Mumma said you can't talk about love in the context of a dog. A dog is just doing its thing. 'But I can love Shortlegs?' I said.

'You can,' Mumma says, 'and you do.'

When Mumma says 'if anyone asks' about Granda, or Ben, or anything else, who she really means is Lucy. Here in the country Lucy is classified as a neighbour, even though she lives three fields away. Lucy's the same age as me but Mumma says she's old for her years. The way she says it, it doesn't sound like a good thing. Lucy can't come in the house but sometimes, after home-schooling, we're allowed to play outdoors at a safe distance. Lucy wanted to know if I missed Glasgow. I asked her if she meant: miss it because it's what I was used to; or miss it because I wish I was there. Mumma talked to me about the difference. 'Miss it because you wish you were there,' Lucy said, 'instead of stuck in this dump!' I told her: I miss going to the cinema whenever we felt like it, and I miss stopping for ice cream on the way home, and I miss Calum and Tess and Corinne, but even if we were there now we couldn't do those things. And if I was in Glasgow, I wouldn't have Shortlegs. I don't think I can give up Shortlegs now.

It was Lucy who took me to see the green cave. It's in the riverbank in the glen behind the house where a spruce tree fell backwards into the forest, and pulled up the soft ground at its base. It must have happened years ago, because the roots are all overgrown with moss and red lichen, and underneath, where the trunk's fallen back, they've formed a perfect cave. It sort of looks like the earth yawned and then froze in that position, like Mumma used to say my mouth would when I made a face. Sometimes when I'm in there, I imagine I can hear the earth breathing, and that the mouth is going to close again and shut me and Shortlegs inside. That's where I go to practice stillness and confinement, in preparation for the space programme. I'm getting really good at it. There are two dry ways into the green cave: you can climb over the top of the roots and lie down on your belly and wiggle backwards till your legs hang over the opening, and then lower yourself down by the arms and swing in, like a chimpanzee; or you can leap over from the opposite riverbank and duck and sort of roll in, commando-style. It's a bit muddy at the mouth of the green cave near the water but farther in it's dry and mossy and above your head the white roots of the tree hang down like crooked fingers. Shortlegs doesn't bother with either of those methods; she wades in through the water and gives herself a good shake once she's inside. It's the best cave in the world. You couldn't make a better one if you tried, and the best part is that no one made it, except the wind that blew over the tree.

Lucy wanted to know where my Dad was. I told her I

haven't got a Dad. She said everyone's got one, or had one, that he might be dead or in Scotland but that I must have had one to begin with. I told her what Mumma told me—that she wanted a child and she got one. 'Are you sperm bank?' Lucy said.

'No. Mumma's Komodo dragon. They can reproduce by themselves.' I looked it up on the internet. I know all about parthenogenesis. Some female sharks can do it too, and the New Mexico whiptail and the queen honeybee.

'She's not a dragon,' Lucy said. 'What about her boyfriend?'

'Who do you mean?'

'Ben Sheridan.'

I laughed out loud at that. 'Ben's not Mumma's boyfriend.'

'What is he then?'

'He's an essential caregiver.'

Lucy's eyes widened. 'He's a farmer,' she said.

'You can be a farmer and a caregiver.'

Lucy shrugged. 'He's nice, but he's too young for your mother anyway.'


Ben lives in the next farm along, in the Clearys' old place. He didn't live there when Mumma was growing up but when the Clearys died, they left the place to him. My granny is dead as well. I never met her. There was a falling out, Mumma said. Granny didn't agree with Mumma's choices. 'Was I one of the choices she didn't agree with?' I asked her and Mumma said I was. 'I'm glad I never met her,' I said. Mumma stroked my hair and said she should have brought me to see her, even though Granny was cross with her, that that was one of her few regrets. Granny would have loved me if she'd met me, Mumma said, she wouldn't have been able to help herself. 'Does Granda love me?' I asked Mumma and a little ripple crossed her face.

'Of course he does,' she said. 'He loves us both. Though sometimes it's hard to tell.'

Mumma and me came to stay with Granda, when he first got out of hospital. It was meant to be for a few days, while his care package was sorted out, but then we had Lockdown and we're still here. Now I take lessons online and Mumma works in the evenings, after she's put me and Granda to bed. I hear her sometimes when I wake up at night, talking to people all around the world, trying to solve their technology problems. Some problems are easier solved than others, Mumma says.

Some weekends, Mumma and me play a trick on Granda, but it's not a cruel trick. When we're at the Spar, we pick up three of their ready meals: cottage pie with extra gravy for Granda; Thai green chicken curry with noodles for us. We go home and clatter about in the kitchen with saucepans and crockery, and dance to Gladys while the meals are heating up in the microwave, then we put the food on plates in the oven to keep warm while we get Granda settled at the table. We keep some back in case Granda says he'll have another scoop out of the pie dish, but Shortlegs loves it when Granda doesn't say that because then she gets to eat the rest. Granda doesn't like curry or noodles or anything with garlic in it— or chillies, he really objects to chillies—so this is our little trick on him. He gets the dinner he wants and so do we, not a single saucepan used.

Shortlegs has a coat the colour of ploughed soil and a white bib and white socks and a white tip to her tail. Her body's too long for the length of her legs. She looks like a big dog that's been cut off at the knees. Ben gave her to Granda when his dog, Spritzer, had a litter, so we know she's part Springer and you can tell that when she bounds through the long meadow between Granda's house and the sea, so that only her head bobs up above the grass. The rest of her, Ben says, is a mystery. His neighbour to the lower end has a boy beagle and up the road there's a Jack Russell and a Dachshund. Ben watches Shortlegs for traits of those other dogs but he says it could have been any one of them that did the business with Spritzer.

This is the list of things that Shortlegs does not like or is afraid of: wheelbarrows; bicycles; tractors; the bin lorry; the post van; walking frames and sticks; wheelchairs; motorbikes; surf boards; ironing boards; kites; kayaks; boats; doorbells; umbrellas (open or closed); helicopters; thunder; lightning and big men (except for Ben).

This is the list of things that Shortlegs likes: running; fetching; sleeping in the sun; belly scratches; gravy; dog biscuits; scrambled egg; boiled rice; meat of any kind; toast; drinking from puddles; prawn crackers; stripping the felt off tennis balls with her teeth, and cooling her feet in the sea. I was worried that the likes were fewer than the dislikes and the fears and that that meant she was sad or afraid more of the time than she was happy or content but Mumma said it doesn't mean that because the likes are more frequent. She has some of what Mumma calls 'strange behaviours'.

She won't eat her food unless you stand over her while she's eating, and she barks at the wind and at aeroplane contrails. She's quieter now that there aren't so many flights in the sky. I told Ben she howled at the North Star and he said, was I sure that that's what it was? I showed him and he said to keep an eye on it: if it was bright when there were no other stars around, and if it moved position across the sky, then it could be the space station, he said, and I checked and it was and it did. It's strange to think of the astronauts up there, circling the earth, confined in their bubble, safe, looking down at us. Ben said he wouldn't blame Shortlegs for barking. He said, 'Who knows what she can sense out there that we can't?'

Granda is what Mumma calls 'set in his ways'. That's what she says when we're in the Spar and people ask after him but sometimes, to Ben, when she thinks I'm not listening, she says he'd drive you round the bend. He was always contrary, she says, but the stroke has made him worse. Now one small irritation can put him in bad form for the whole day. Mumma has cut all the labels off his shirts and sweaters so they don't scratch his neck, and all the cuffs off his thermals so they don't suffocate his ankles. When your world is as small as Granda's has become everything in it is bigger and itchier and tighter. I worry about this now that all our worlds have shrunk. I think if my world was as small as Granda's, I would want everything in it to be just as I liked it too, including the tiny yoghurt and the blue eggcup and the twelve apostles' spoons.

Granny collected the full set of the apostles' spoons, including Judas, though Mumma says she wasn't much fussed about him. Granda doesn't mind what order they come in, so long as we never give him the same spoon twice in one day. To be on the safe side, I lay them all out on the shelf in the 'spare things' cupboard where Granda's tablets are kept, and select them from left to right and put the used one back at the end of the row. This morning it's Saint James the Lesser. I always feel sorry for him. Just because there were two Jameses doesn't mean that one has to be lesser than the other, because he was younger, or shorter, maybe, than the other James. His symbol is a club because he was beaten to death. The Bible is a violent place. We never bothered with it much in Scotland but everyone's very interested in it here. Granda has a huge Bible, with a cream fake leather cover, and gilt edges and coloured prints inside. There's a picture of Abraham with his fingers spread over Isaac's face and an ugly, curved blade in his other hand, ready to cut his son's throat, and then the angel at his shoulder, saying it's all right; you can stop now—it was a test—just in time to save him. Imagine if the angel had been three seconds late? I don't like the pictures but I can't stop myself from going back to look. Granny bought the Bible off a salesman, Mumma said, and paid it in every week. Mumma's name is in the front under Granny's and Granda's names and my two great-grannies' names and my great-grandas' names, but they didn't put my name in. It's because I wasn't christened, Mumma said, but then she wrote my name in herself, and I added Shortlegs's name too. I reckon that makes Shortlegs my next of kin. Mumma is Granda's next of kin. That's why the hospital rang her when Granda took the stroke. But she wasn't down as Granny's next of kin so they didn't ring her the time Granny got ill and that's how we missed the funeral. Mumma was sad when she found out, but she says she's forgiven Granda now.

'Matthew, Mark, Luke and John, God Bless the bed that I lie on, and if I die before I wake, I pray to God my soul to take.' Granda says this as soon as he sees the apostle's spoon, and then he empties his tablets from the blue eggcup into the tiny yoghurt and crunches his way through the lot. Mumma says this is a bedtime prayer but Granda can't help himself: the apostle's spoon sets him off every time. I asked Mumma where Granda thinks God will take his soul when he dies and Mumma said, to heaven, he hopes, where Granny will be.

'Is she?' I asked Mumma.

'Is she what?'

'Is Granny in Heaven?'

'That's what Granda believes,' Mumma said. 'And you'd think he would know. They were married for fifty-one years.'

'I'll wave over at her,' I said, 'on my way to Mars.'

I watched a programme on TV about Mars, about the polar ice caps where it snows carbon dioxide and about the ancient salt deposits and the places where they believe water used to flow. So far, NASA has only managed to land a rover there, but the programme narrator said that the person could be alive today who would walk on the surface of the red planet. It would take seven earth months to get there, but you could set up home in a lava tube in a volcano, not that different from the green cave, and sit out the dust storms under a natural skylight, and watch a Martian sunset. I told

Mumma that that person could be me and she said, 'Why not? For you, Cassie, not even the sky is the limit.'

Mars has two small potato-shaped moons. Some scientists think it may once have had a third moon, whose orbit finally eroded. They think that when the lost moon collided with Mars, the impact may have formed the *Orcus Patera* crater. I measured my orbit and I measured Mumma's and I measured Shortlegs's and Granda's too. If you include Glasgow, and France that time we went on holiday, then my orbit, before Lockdown, was nine hundred and ten miles and I reckon Mumma's was about the same. Now me and Mumma have the same orbit as Shortlegs, which is about three miles and takes in the Spar and the green cave and the sea, though Shortlegs covers at least four times that distance every time we go out, because she runs backwards and forwards to me. Granda can only go from his armchair to the kitchen table, or to the bathroom, or to his bed. If you take the TV as the central point, I reckon his orbit is about twenty steps, and he can't always make those on his own. He doesn't lift his knees up high enough; he slides his feet along the carpet after his walking frame. It's like gravity has a stronger pull on him than it does on the rest of us. We have to keep an eye on him when he's moving around. Granda's speed is very low but all the same, I watch him for signs of collision, in case the same thing happens to him that happened with the missing Martian moon.

Me and Granda and Shortlegs all have the same bedtime. Mumma helps Granda to change into his pyjamas and I put Shortlegs in the back porch and then I leave everything out ready for the morning. After he's had his tablets, Granda likes a swig of water from the Famous Grouse glass (half from the pump, half from the kettle to take the chill off) and then he turns his eggcup upside down so he knows that that part's over and the next part is porridge. Apart from the apostles' spoons, Granda can hardly remember what he's done three seconds ago, but some days, he can remember sinking the well for the pump and the white sand that filled the hole, fine enough to run through an hour glass, and he can remember building the wall of the boiler house and great-granda teaching him how to use the shotgun and he tells me all about these things. He remembers when his own granny lived in the lower end of the house with a door that faced the front when their door faced the back so that there were two houses the exact same, joined together, but facing in opposite directions, like two pieces of Lego. But he doesn't always remember who I am. 'Kitty,' he says when he looks at me, and then 'Catherine,' and then, 'Cassie', at last. He can't always get to me without passing through Granny and Mumma first.

Now the two side-by-side houses are one long narrow house and Granda sleeps in the end that his Granny used to live in, behind the chimney, for heat, and near the bathroom, for convenience. Mumma and me have a room each at the other end, mine at the front, Mumma's at the back, with the living room and the kitchen in the middle. When Granda's settled, Mumma comes in to read to me. I try to stay awake on Saturdays to hear Ben coming in but sometimes I fall asleep and miss him. Sometimes Ben tells me stories of what our grandas got up to when they were young, when they rode to the dances on their bicycles and tried to sneak in without paying. When they were 'coortin', Ben said.

'What's "coortin"?' I asked him.

'You know, when he was going out with your Granny.'

I find it hard to picture Granda on a bicycle. His orbit at that time must have been miles and miles and miles.

Last night, I must have fallen asleep early because I didn't hear Ben coming in. I woke up and the room was dark, with just the light from the hall coming under the door. I knew that something had woken me, but I didn't know what it was. I pulled back the curtain and looked out the window to the front of the house but it was cloudy and dark outside. And then I heard a noise down the hall. I got up and went into the living room but it was empty and the playing cards were laid out, face-down on the green table and Ben's empty glass was beside them and then I heard the noise again, coming from Granda's room. I walked down the hall and pushed the door open and Granda was lying crumpled on his side on the floor, and he was moaning, and there was a bad smell in the room. I switched on the light and shouted for Mumma and went to Granda but when I tried to take his elbow he yelled at me and flung out his arm and his knuckle caught me on the side of the face. I shouted for Mumma again and then again, and then she was there, finally, with Ben behind her. She ran to Granda, was asking was he all right, had he broken anything, could he get up, and then—this was the worst thing—Granda started to cry. And Mumma said, 'It's okay, Daddy, you're all right, I'm here now,' and Granda said 'Kitty?' and kept on crying and I could tell that Mumma felt like crying too but there was something else, because her face was red and her hair was all tossed, and whatever the name for it was, Ben was that as well. Then Mumma said they'd need to lift Granda and: 'Will you get me an old towel, Cassie?' she said, so I ran and grabbed one of Shortlegs's towels from the bottom of the hot press. 'Put it over the bed,' she said. Then she and Ben hoisted Granda up on to the mattress between them and rolled him on to his side. Mumma started tugging at the waist of Granda's pyjama bottoms, trying to pull them out from under him, and the smell was getting worse.

I didn't really want to stay but there was something bothering me. 'Where were you?' I said to Mumma.

'What?' she said, still tugging at Granda's pyjamas.

'I was calling for you and you didn't come.'

She kept her head down. 'The living room,' she said.

'You weren't.'

'We were! Or—we must have been outside when you looked—we stepped out for a minute—to look at the stars.'

Ben had his face turned away from me, was reaching over Granda's shoulder, holding him on his side while my mother struggled to roll the pyjamas down Granda's trapped legs. I could see dark stains all down Granda's thermals and the smell was horrible, but still I stayed.

'You weren't outside. I looked,' I said. Her face turned redder still and she stopped what she was doing and she looked straight at me.

'Cassie!' she said. 'If you can't be any help then just go back to bed!'

'Granda hit me,' I said.

Mumma's face collapsed. She took a step towards me, 'Oh, Cassie, let me see.' Then she looked down at her hands and said, 'Give me a minute. I just have to sort Granda out first, okay?'

I looked at Ben but he was still turned away from me. I left Granda's room and went out through the kitchen into the back porch and sat down on the tiles with my back to the wall. I could hear Mumma talking to Granda, saying he'd be all right, they'd have him sorted in no time; he wasn't to get upset. Shortlegs roused herself and stretched her back legs and crept up on to my knee. I scratched her ears and rubbed her belly and she curled her back right into my stomach and rubbed her face with her paws and normally that cheers me right up but it didn't make me feel any better this time. The tiles were cold through my pyjamas and my cheek was stinging still. I could feel a lump starting to rise on the bone. Mumma never shouts at me. Mumma never cries. 'So this is what a collision feels like,' I said to Shortlegs. It turns out that a body doesn't need to be travelling all that fast for you to feel the impact when it hits. I craned my neck to see outside, through the stippled glass in the porch door, but we were facing the wrong way for the space station and there wasn't a single star in the sky.

# In the Interests of Wonder

What kind of day is it, the day the magician knocks on the schoolroom door? May time, before the early fair, foxglove and fuchsia in the hedges, flag irises on the fringes of the lakes. He cycles up the steep hill that rises out of the bay, upright on the pedals, coat-tails flying, without any loss of breath. His daughter sails on the handlebars, expertly balanced, of course.

The children in the schoolroom are fidgety at their desks, restless to be outdoors. What does he hear as he stands outside? The voice of the teacher and the voices of the children, lifting and falling like blossom on the breeze, questions and answers on their Catechism. 'What are the twelve fruits of the Holy Spirit, Alice Rooney? What is the meaning of the word "Amen"? And what, James Boyd, is Hell?' It is days from their Confirmation and still they do not know and it will be her head on the block if they're turned from the altar rails. How long does the magician stand there outside, waiting, listening to her threaten and scold, all the time holding his daughter by the hand?

When the teacher, finally, hears the knock and opens the door to them he is courteous, removes his hat, stands silent for a moment to allow her to take him in: the embroidered waistcoat, the butterfly collar at his throat. His hair is braided behind each ear and the many braids fall to his shoulders. His eyebrows are very straight. He has brought a playbill, asks if he may post it where the children will see it. 'Delightful Illusions,' it reads. 'Inimitable and Marvellous Feats.' The teacher is aware of the children at her back, straining to catch a glimpse of the strangers. She takes the bill from his hand. His gaze lingers on the fineness of her fingers, drifts to her narrow waist. The performance is suitable for the young, he says, he takes nothing to do with the black arts, with coarseness or impropriety. The girl peers around him, eyes the children seated in rows at their desks. She is wearing a home-made dress, sandals, bright white socks. Her hair is neat and ribboned. Her hands and face are clean, her cheeks a little pink from the cycle.

'My assistant,' he says, tugging the child forward. 'She would benefit from some extra tuition. Do you speak French?' A diamond stud on his shirt front, a cravat of red and gold.

'No, sir. I'm afraid I do not.'

'That's a shame. French would be useful. Still, arithmetic, verbal reasoning: those are useful too. She has missed some of her schooling.'

'Mr...?'

He flutters the playbill, performs a small bow. 'Wyatt The Wonder, Monsieur Gazon, The Professor Merveilleux.'

'Which is it?' she asks him.

He waves his hand. 'Take your pick,' he says. His accent, an American twang.

'It must be tiring,' she nods at the poster, 'being superlative, in such a variety of guises.'

'To some people, perhaps,' he says. 'To others, excellence

comes naturally. You'll come to the house?'

'We haven't discussed terms.'

'But you'll come,' he says. 'You know where we are.' He turns with the girl by the hand.

She does know, of course. The whole village knows. They heard that the doctor had let the Cave House. They watched the troupe arrive on the Saturday before. The group rolled up in three trucks, the first painted in black lacquer, a poster of the magician, collared and moustachioed, pasted on to the side. In the picture a little sprite sat on his shoulder, whispered secrets in his ear. 'Direct From The Home Of Mystery,' it read. 'The Country's Foremost Illusionist.' Which country, it did not say. He was a worldwide sensation, a natural wonder. 'Strange Peregrinations,' the poster proclaimed: 'Classical Prestidigitation. Prepare For A Succession of Surprises'. The surprise, the teacher was thinking, as she turned with her basket from the grocer's, was in the number of syllables employed, the meaning left suitably vague. The posters, when she looked a little closer, seemed oddly cropped, like they had originally been part of a larger playbill, like this modest troupe had been annexed from a much grander show.

The second of the vehicles was a stake-bed truck with rattling cages and canvases. The third was a sort of caravan, a room on wheels the like of which she had never seen. They rattled over the bridge, made their way past the hotel, towards the mouth of the harbour and up the climb to the caves. But they hadn't reckoned on the narrowness of the entrance, the low overhanging rock. The cavalcade stopped while the three drivers conferred. The spectacle drew a crowd. Jim Foley emerged from the doorway of the hotel, nodded at the teacher: 'Miss McDonnell,' he said. Hands jiggling in his trousers pockets, hair combed back behind his ears. He took up position at the gable of the hotel, said something out of the side of his mouth to his stalwart, Paudie Kane. Kane in a flat cap and tie, knitted sweater, laughed and peered down the street, into the sunlight, to the spot where the trucks had pulled up.

The first driver, a burly man in white shirt and suspenders, thought he could get the vehicle through by going easy, keeping to the middle of the path. The truck inched through. A lazy cheer went up from those who had gathered. The second truck wedged fast. They had to let the air out of the tyres. Foley and Kane were among the men who lined up behind and began to push. From the back a cacophony of quacking and squawking but then the truck was through to the other side and the third, the magician behind the wheel, passed too and they disappeared from sight.

The day is clear and bright on the afternoon the teacher locks up the schoolroom for the day and walks through the caves. The sandstone walls are packed with boulders. You can see the places where the stones have come free, leaving empty sockets the size of a child's skull. Through the gate, the rocks that border the gravel path are cushioned green with moss and lichen. Elder trees arch overhead. The house is hidden by a steep green bank to the right; the sea hinted at by an opening in the rock to the left.

The path opens on to a green lawn, a scattering of tents, the short burly man from the first truck, now balancing on a unicycle, his legs pedalling back and forth. The wheel wobbles, he throws back his head, juggles six coloured balls high into the air. Down there on the shore the girl is paddling in the clear water, staring down between her feet, her dress knotted at the back of her knees. A woman, a thick-set person in her middle years, sits on a sheltered seat against a garden wall, her head bent over some sewing. As the teacher approaches, the magician appears at the door of the house, sleeves rolled up, collarless now, shirt unbuttoned at the throat: 'Esmée!' he calls. The girl turns her head. 'Come! Your tutor is here.'

Follow the teacher into a bright room, to a faded rug, six chairs, a polished mahogany table. Watch as she puts down her satchel, and walks to the window as the girl strolls up the lawn, her shoes and socks in her hand. Esmée is eleven or twelve, maybe, with a sun browned face, dark hair curled down her back.

'You're tall for a woman,' says the magician. It's not the first time the teacher has heard this.

She turns towards him. 'How tall is a woman required to be?'

'Five foot three inches. What do you weigh?'

'A hundred and twelve pounds.'

He raises an eyebrow. 'So precise. How can you be sure?'

'My father uses me as a counterweight when he's filling bags of potatoes.'

He looks at her, a little uncertain, then his mouth curls into a smile. 'Your father is a farmer, I think, like my own?'

'Your father is a farmer?' The news surprises her.

'In one of his lives,' he says.

She must look startled. He smiles again. 'That is an almost perfect weight. Ideally, you don't want to be more than a hundred and ten pounds.'

'You have very specific requirements, sir.'

'For the illusion I'm working on,' he says. 'The Vanishing Lady needs to be supple, her limbs need to bend in all the right places. She needs to be able to fit into a very tight spot.' He glances at the bones of her wrist, at her pliable waist.

'How many ladies have you vanished?' she asks him.

'A few,' he says. 'Some several times over. They nearly always come back.'

'The child's mother?' she says, though it is none of her business. These are the days of teachers asking anything they like.

'Dead,' he says. A twitch in the corner of his eye.

The teacher looks out at the woman on the bench, dark hair scraped back, busy sewing, a benign expression on her face.

'The child's grandmother,' the magician says. 'You have lived here all of your life?' he asks then. 'In this one place?'

'Yes.'

He looks around, at the sea, back towards the village, the hotel, the little schoolhouse on the hill. 'What do you do for love?' he says, the way another person might ask, 'what do you do for fuel in the winter?' or 'what do you do for fresh vegetables when your own are done?'

She looks away from him. She is thinking, perhaps, of the proposition that Jim Foley has put to her, only a fortnight before. Is there love in that? Could there ever be?

'I don't need to see a person's eyes to read their thoughts,' the magician says.

Esmée is a quiet, serious child. She concentrates hard on her studies, does her lessons as required. They come to an agreement, the magician and the teacher. She goes to the Cave House three times a week, after she finishes in the schoolhouse. The magician is sometimes there, on the periphery, sometimes he stays out of their way. She does not enquire into the mysteries of their lives, into the business of what happens onstage. But one day, during an arithmetic lesson, when they are discussing the concept of infinity, the child reaches out her arm. She says: 'Feel that, Miss. I am solid, am I not? Skin and flesh and bone. When I perform as my father's assistant, I am astonished that the people in the audience believe I am capable of disappearing. Where do they think I go?'

'The people in the audience are willing accomplices,' the teacher tells her. 'They are paying to be fooled. They cannot figure out how the tricks are done and they want to see them done again.'

'He is very clever, my father,' the girl nods. 'The audience gasps and whoops and applauds. They come back again and again.'

'He is very successful?' the teacher says. She has been wondering why he has come here.

'He is the best,' says Esmée. 'And now I'm good too. I am not scared. Even though the audience can't see me, I know that I am still here.'

'That's good,' says the teacher. 'That's important.'

'I could teach you,' the girl says.

A laugh. 'I don't see the need.'

'It could be useful. My mother was very good at disappearing. She disappeared all the time, even when she wasn't supposed to. My father says that this time, she's never coming back. But I don't know how he can be so sure. Sometimes she stayed away for a very long time but she always came back in the end.'

There is a pause. The teacher remains silent. What is she to say?

'She has very beautiful dresses,' Esmée says. 'She left them all with us. I don't think she would have done that if she didn't intend to come back. I'm going to be just like her. I'm going to disappear too.' She goes back to her calculations. 'I am The Indestructible Girl,' she says, 'I am The Long Acre Ghost. I am The Living Pincushion. I can Pass Through The Eye Of A Needle.'

'Who is your father?' the teacher asks her.

'He is Wyatt The Wondrous; he is The Man Of A Thousand Tricks; he is The Man Without A Middle. The show is nearly ready. When are you coming to see it?'

On the almost empty stage of the parish hall stands a wooden table supported by five ornate elephant heads, their trunks pointing down, forming a lattice beneath. In the wings can be seen a lacquered cabinet, painted with alligators, black, red, green and gold. The magician appears pushing an empty rickshaw, like a Roman chariot, with two huge wooden wheels. He has kohled his eyes for the performance. He wears a dark velvet cloak, tied at the throat, bordered with silk, a shirt that is finished with pearls. Above the contraption, like a circular sunshade, is a furled curtain which he lowers via a tasselled cord. There are words, gestures, the eyes of the audience on him, on the lowered curtain. There is no movement from within. He walks around it, pulls the cord, the curtain rises and there is Esmée, seated, smiling, in a fur-trimmed dress, appeared from who knows where. He offers his hand, the girl takes it, steps down on to the stage, as if this were the most natural thing in the world. He looks a little pained, like he wishes it weren't necessary for his daughter to do this. His hands, long-fingered, expressive as speech, are very white under the lights. His hair shines with oil.

The hall is packed. The Benson twins in matching plaid caps, lean forward clutching at the seats in front for support. They must be near ninety the pair of them, bent in the middle at the same point, just below the second button of their jackets. The one cannot go anywhere without the other for fear of missing out. Fat Feeley is in some kind of cowboy hat, wherever he got his hands on it, his belly hanging over his belt, the strain on his shirt buttons almost unbearable to witness. His fiddle-shaped wife sits proud beside him, narrow-bosomed, wide-hipped, a neck long enough to play on, if you could have found the means to string it, a face full of frets you would happily retune if you thought it would produce a smile. Their youngest girl, Marjorie, clings to her mother, arms cinched around her waist, but all the while with her face turned sideways coveting the yellow bouncing curls of Sarah Stewart. Ade Fullerton, in the row in front is sharp-chinned, brooding with rage, like a boy who is always scheming. And there is poor Jenny Miller with her twisted mouth, her chin sticky with sugar, cardigan pockets sagging with buttons and coins, a vacant look on her face.

The show continues: rabbits appear; ducks vanish; the business of the elephant head table goes on. But the scale is not quite right for two performers on a small provincial stage. The furniture, the effects are oversized. They are dwarfed, the magician and his daughter, by the ghost of a much more sensational show, the shadows of acrobats on slack wires, the echoes of a band of horn players, the remembered sparkle of dancers in bejewelled bodices, diaphanous robes. They are like orphans, the two of them, exiles from under a larger canvas which carries on somewhere without them, still big in their minds. Esmée does not speak. The magician throws two coloured plates into the air and she catches and spins them on a rod that she passes behind her back. He throws two more; with a second rod in her other hand, she catches these too, balances both on her chin. The plates tremble like trapped butterflies three feet above her head. Her eyes are glued to them the entire time. 'Dancing Delph' he says to the audience and bows. The audience applauds the girl.

The magician makes walking sticks dance of their own accord. He produces a bouquet of flowers from under his hat. He raises the elephant table at the tips of his fingers and it levitates in the air. He passes a white handkerchief through a sparkling tube and lo! the handkerchief turns red, then yellow, then green, then blue. 'Cheap tricks!' shouts a voice from the back of the audience. His left eye twitches. He is playing for time.

He asks for a wedding ring. Mrs Duddy passes up

hers. 'That'll be the last you'll see of that,' shouts Jimmy McPhellimy from a few rows back. The magician folds a playbill in half, then folds the sides to create a paper bag. He drops the ring in and takes a hammer to it, battering the ring out of shape. Mrs Duddy squeaks, clasps her hand to her bosom. The magician tears up the bag. The ring has disappeared. He hands the tattered pieces of paper to Mrs Duddy to hold. She rifles through the fragments for her ring and finds none. He conjures a newly laid egg out of the air. He cracks open the egg: a canary appears. On a ribbon around the bird's neck hangs Mrs Duddy's ring, uninjured, shining, as the day twenty years ago when Mr Duddy first slipped it on to her finger. He asks Mrs Duddy for the shreds of paper. As she passes them back, they burst into flame and fall as ash to the stage. He waves his hand, blows out the flame, in his fist is the playbill he originally tore, intact. The audience gapes. He returns the ring. Esmée sets the canary on a perch in its cage. Cage and canary disappear.

She knows it's not real but the teacher can't figure out how it's done. She is watching him as closely as she can. 'Legerdemain,' the doctor says down the row from her: 'Impeccable sleight-of-hand. We see what the magician chooses for us to see.'

'What delight we take in being duped,' Mrs Duddy trills.

Without witnesses, his feats have no currency; without the performance, they feel lesser, bereft. Where did it go their sense of wonder? At what point in their lives did they lose it? For an hour or two, they remember what it is to be astonished.

In the applause that follows the magician asks for a volunteer and Jenny Miller jumps up off her seat, pockets jangling, wiping her chin on her cardigan sleeve and waves her hand in the air. Jenny and the teacher were inseparable as children. People used to say they looked alike, before Jenny took the fall that damaged her head. The magician glances at her, hesitates. The teacher watches him calculate the worth of the trick, pitching the value of entertainment against an assessment of risk, working out how far he can reasonably go with a subject such as Jenny. He shakes his head but it does not matter. Jim Foley has caught Jenny by the arm, is saying, 'Sit down, girl,' is already climbing the wooden steps to the stage. The magician places Foley on a chair, facing the audience, says he is going to hypnotise him. Is Foley willing? he asks. He is, Foley says. Foley pushes up his sleeves, veins bulging in his forearms, as if physical strength were a match for the magician's skill. He asks Foley to close his eyes and when his eyes are shut, the magician produces a pencil from behind his ear. He tells Foley he is holding a red-hot poker and with the pencil he touches Foley's bare arm. Foley flinches, as if he has been branded. Next the magician tells him the pencil is a feather and this time Foley squirms and giggles at the touch. 'Tell him it's your tool,' shouts the Piper Loaney from the back of the hall, full of meths as usual, and they can still hear the roars of him as big John Carey marches him out the door by his ear.

When the fuss dies down, the magician hands Foley a glass of water and tells him it is bitter medicine. Foley takes a sip, screws up his face, refuses a second drink. He tells him the same glass is lemonade and Foley swallows it in one draught, smacks his lips and smiles. What kind of power does he have over perception that he can fool a person in this way? They look into Foley's face and they know that he is gone—where they cannot say—and for a moment, they wonder if he'll ever come back and at least one of them wonders how big a loss that would be. And then they look at the magician and they see that he isn't concerned at all. He holds Foley's mind in his hand, as light and as sturdy as an egg. When he deems that the time is right, he hands it back to him, not a crack in it. But they know as he does it that he has the power to smash it and they fear him a little, and are fascinated at once. What would he do with their minds if they were to offer them? Where would he send them?

Foley blinks and shakes himself and looks at the audience laughing and clapping, pounding their feet, then back at the magician again. He smiles, uncertain, staggers back down to his seat. Paudie Kane grabs him by the elbow, laughing into his ear. It is clear that Foley doesn't like what he hears. He shakes Paudie off, grabs his jacket, rises to his feet, strides out the back of the hall. Jenny jumps up and follows after him but soon returns to her seat. They say Jenny went every night after that and asked to be hypnotised every time but the magician always passed over her, chose someone else instead.

During one of their lessons, Esmée says to the teacher, 'Would you like me to read your palm?'

'Is that something you do?'

'My mother taught me.'

'All right.' She stretches her right hand out to the girl. Esmée takes the teacher's fingers in her hand, turns them over in hers.

'Air,' she says. The teacher looks at her blankly. 'The shape of your hand. It indicates,' she pauses, 'a person of the mind.'

'That's fair to say.'

'You are contemplative, slow, perhaps, to action. A person who is comfortable with things that cannot be explained.'

'I'm a teacher. Everything can be explained.'

'So you understand how the illusions work?'

'No.'

'You think my father practises magic?'

'I think your father is practised and skilled. He knows exactly what to do, where to place the sliding sheets of mirror glass, the drapery, the wires, the lights.'

Esmée nods, considering this, looks down again at the hand. 'Air people,' she says, 'don't want to be the same as the people they see around them.'

'Interesting,' the teacher says.

'They are quick-witted.'

'I like this.'

'But they can be spiteful and cold.'

'I like that not so much, although I won't deny that it can occasionally be true.'

'You are a good keeper of secrets.'

'I have no secrets to keep.'

'Of your own, and of others,' the girl says. She looks again at the hand. 'You are not adventurous.'

The teacher laughs aloud. 'What adventures are there to be had here?' she asks.

The girl looks grave. 'There are adventures everywhere.'

'Will I live a long life?' the teacher asks her. 'Isn't that what everyone wants to know?'

'That's not for me to say. What the life line tells is how you live it. You have plenty of energy and vitality.' She pauses. 'You are not easily influenced by others. There have been no sudden changes in your life to date.'

'There have not,' says the teacher, laughing again, 'that is true. Go on.'

'Your fate line doesn't meet your life line.'

'What does that mean?'

'It means that you are not prepared to give up your own interests to those of others.'

'I don't think so.'

'Have it your own way.' She examines the hand again. 'You do not fall in love easily,' she says.

The teacher pulls her hand away. 'What nonsense!'

'So you do fall in love easily?'

'I mean that the whole thing is nonsense. A party trick. How on earth could you tell from a person's hand what their propensity for love will be?'

The girl shrugs. 'It's not just the hand,' she says, 'although the lines are a good indication of what is in the body, the face. My mother fell in love easily,' she says. 'She fell in love anew every day.'

The teacher looks away, out through the window to where the sea ripples on the pebbles, washes in and out.

'Would you like me to continue?'

She gives back her hand.

'You will not have children,' Esmée says.

Here's what the teacher learned about the magician, from Esmée, from watching him, from listening to what he said. He enjoyed a drink: whiskey, mostly. He had demons, plenty of them. He was a smoker: twenty Players a day. He smelled of cigarettes. When he drew on the Players, he put his index and his middle fingers flat against his lips and he blew the smoke out gently. He was a reader. He talked about books. Somewhere, in America, maybe somewhere else, there was a baby he had left behind. He knew a man who believed he could fly, who broke his neck diving from a bridge. He knew how to wrestle a snake. He had met a woman with the skin of an elephant. He had a friend, a man, who hammered nails up his nose. He had seen a boy emerge from the horn of a tuba. He had made a goat disappear. He once drove a truck through a road full of dead fish. He was ringmaster in a wagon circus in Alabama; he was a magician in Hamburg ten years before; he was leader of a company on a Mississippi riverboat; he kept hens in Arkansas. He had performed, he said, for a Sultan in Morocco, for judiciaries in Australia, for property magnates in New York. He was the owner of a magic emporium in Scarborough; he served in the Royal Navy during the war. Who knows where he'd been. He could not be placed. He had no antecedents. He didn't care what anyone thought. 'When I worked on the railroad,' he said once, and even though the teacher looked at him the way she looked at the children when they told a bald untruth, he never broke his stride.

He possessed nine top hats and every one of them must have been six feet deep, judging by the number of scented bouquets and coloured handkerchiefs he kept under there.

He was a chapeaugraphist, a shadowist, a conjurer, a coin manipulator, a juggler, a mechanical wizard, a cardsharp, a mesmerist. He played the cornet. Coins flew from his fingertips. He escaped from fetters with ease. He could not have looked or acted any more differently to the sloppy-jacketed, big-eared men of the village that he came amongst. He had a straight nose. The teacher thought him beautiful. She walked away from him and looked over her shoulder and found her way back again.

And for a man who made his living from deception, he could be very direct.

'Would the priest marry us?' he asked the teacher, one day as she was leaving the house.

'Is that a proposal?' she said.

'If you like.'

'No. He wouldn't. At least not without the proper notice. How could he know you're not married already? How could he know you haven't a dozen wives secreted away?'

'I don't,' he said. 'Would it matter? Would you come with me, if I asked?'

'Is it a wife or an assistant you're looking for?'

'Both,' he said. 'Either.'

'Ask and you'll find out.'

The teacher had never played a game like this where the game was to say what was on your mind and pretend that you were bluffing. At least that's the game that she was playing. She could never tell if it was the same with him.

'We will never have this time again,' he said.

'We won't.'

'Meet me tonight? After the show?'

She didn't say that she wouldn't.

When things go wrong, people look around for something or someone to blame. They don't like to feel powerless, or to feel duped, or to feel that they have been made to look a fool. They think there must be some reason, some triggering or prompting for their misfortunes. And the people there didn't have to look far or long to find the thing that was new, that was changed, that hadn't been there before: the magician and his troupe. When Jake Fullerton began to fail and the weight fell off him like snow off a ditch and the doctor couldn't say what ailed him and food wouldn't stay in his stomach for longer than half an hour and passed straight through him with no gain to him at all, the people said it was on account of the night that the magician passed a sword through his middle. And Phonsie James had a bealing ear that never healed after the magician plucked a coin out of it that time, and whispered whatever it was he had whispered into Phonsie's head. And Mrs Duddy quarrelled with her husband and afterwards said she should never have taken her wedding ring off her finger. And Jim Foley was never easy, said there were whole hours at a time when he couldn't account for himself, after the night the magician had borrowed his brain. And then Jenny disappeared, this time for days together, and when she reappeared it was face-down under one of the arches of the bridge, pale and bloated with her eyes wide open and her belly full of river water, and a scraping of skin under her nails.

And everyone began to ask questions about where Jenny had been and who she'd been with, and what hour of the day that had been. And Jim Foley said he couldn't be sure, but one night he was coming out of the hotel, he thought he saw her, leaving the hall, late on after everyone else had left. So they went to the magician and they questioned him and he said he knew nothing about Jenny. And they said, prove that you weren't with her and he said they'd have to speak to the teacher. And they climbed the hill and the father said, 'What are you doing here? Go away: she's had nothing to do with him.' And when they went back the magician was already gone, disappeared, him and his daughter and his whole troupe, into the air. And the teacher couldn't decide which was worse: that she had betrayed him, or that he knew she would.

The teacher's father met her late on the lane the night she was coming home from the hall. She was pushing the bicycle along the rutted track, the lamp flickering off and on when he stepped out in front of her, his bulk in the light of the yard. The next thing she knew was his hand on her arm, his other on the handlebar. 'Have you no respect, for yourself, for your family? A woman of your years, of your standing in the community? Put any notion of that man out of your head,' he said. The teacher pulled away from him. She said she would do what she liked, that she wasn't beholden to him. 'What do you think will happen?' he said. 'Has he promised that he'll marry you? Is that what you're hoping for? Tell that to the women in those other places, left holding his babies. Catch yourself on, woman. I know a cur when I see one. He's making a fool of you.' And maybe it was because it was him that was saying it, he who would certainly recognise that lack in another man, that made her slow her steps. The teacher's father is rumoured to have fathered at least three other children—children he has never acknowledged and whom she herself has taught, children who have looked at her with his eyes over slates and copy books smudged with ink, unaware of their connection, that they are being instructed by their half-sister. She had had her doubts about the magician, but she'd pushed them all aside, for want of a life without rote answers, for want of breathing new air. Her father saved her from disgrace. Her father saved her from love.

Jim Foley came and spoke to her father and her father spoke to her. Foley offered to take her off his hands, despite what he knew about her. She said she preferred to be a teacher. She said married life wouldn't suit her. Her father couldn't make her take Foley. And it suited him well enough to have a slave in the house.

The magician could make a person do anything he wanted them to do. 'It's a responsibility,' he used to say. But he never did that to her. He never once made her do a thing she didn't want to do. And even after her father said what he said, if the magician had come to her and asked her the question, she'd have followed him anywhere.

Another May, another class, another Confirmation. The children lift their faces and recite the familiar words. The teacher's father has fallen ill. He is almost blind. His mouth is covered in sores. His head aches; his body is limp; they say he raves in his sleep. The doctor tells the teacher her father's heart is weak; it won't be long till he's gone. She nods her head in a gesture that the doctor takes for sorrow.

'The word "Amen",' the children say in the schoolroom

on the hill, 'means "So be it," Miss. Hell is a place or state of punishment… of everlasting suffering… The twelve fruits of the Holy Spirit are: charity; joy; peace; kindness; goodness; generosity; gentleness; faithfulness; modesty; self-control; chastity…'

'What have you forgotten, now?' the teacher says. 'Perhaps the most important one of all?'

They count on their fingers, look to one another, strain hard to remember. Then, relieved to have landed on the missing word:

'Patience, Miss, patience,' they say.

And the teacher nods and smiles and says, 'Patience. Good. Well remembered. And now it's time for the sins.'

# Acknowledgements

Thank you to the Arts Council of Northern Ireland and to the National Lottery for financial support over the last couple of years. Particular thanks to Damian Smyth. Thank you to the Royal Literary Fund for training and employment opportunities. Thank you to David Torrans, Emma Warnock, Stephen Connolly and the entire team at No Alibis Press for their work and for their faith in this collection. Thank you to all the writing friends, online and off, who have kept the conversation going and to Paul Maddern at the River Mill Writers' Retreat. Thank you to Kevin, Mary and Rosie for their forbearance, and to Spooky, aka Shortlegs, for making us laugh and keeping us (sort of) sane.

Thank you to the editors and publishers of the publications in which a number of these stories first appeared.

'There is More than One Word': *Belfast Stories*, edited by Paul McVeigh and Lisa Frank, Doire Press, Galway, 2019.

'A Loss': *The Black Dreams*, edited by Reggie Chamberlain-King, Blackstaff Press, Belfast, 2021.

'The Escapologist': first published in *Fortnight* magazine, literary editor Anne Devlin, July 2021.

'Glass Girl': *Female Lines*, edited by Linda Anderson & Dawn Miranda Sherratt-Bado, New Island Books, Dublin, 2017, and in the paperback edition of *The Watch House*, Tinder Press, London, 2018.

'A Fuss': *The Long Gaze Back: An Anthology of Irish Women Writers*, edited by Sinéad Gleeson, New Island Books, Dublin, 2015 (winner of the Best Irish-Published Book at Bord Gáis Energy Irish Book Awards in 2015).

'The Cure for Too Much Feeling': *The Glass Shore: Short Stories by Women Writers from the North of Ireland*, edited by Sinéad Gleeson, New Island Books, Dublin, 2016 (winner of the Best Irish-Published Book at Bord Gáis Energy Irish Book Awards in 2016).

'Nomad': *Her Other Language: Northern Irish Women Writers Address Domestic Violence and Abuse*, edited by Ruth Carr and Natasha Cuddington, Arlen House, Dublin, 2020.

'Star Gazers': extract published as 'Small Steps' in *Reading the Future: New Writing from Ireland Celebrating 250 Years of Hodges Figgis*, edited by Alan Hayes, Arlen House, Dublin, 2018.